Tag, We're It (A Reverse Harem Dark Romance)

Not-So Childish Games
Duet Book 2

TRIS WYNTERS
Kayla Englert

Tris Wynters Publishing

CONTENTS

CONTENT & TRIGGER WARNINGS - vii
DEDICATION - xi
PLAYLIST - xiii

~Chapter 1~
1

~Chapter 2~
6

~Chapter 3~
12

~Chapter 4~
14

~Chapter 5~
21

~Chapter 6~
27

~Chapter 7~
31

~Chapter 8~
38

~Chapter 9~
41

~Chapter 10~
47

~Chapter 11~
60

~Chapter 12~
63

~Chapter 13~
66

~Chapter 14~
73

~Chapter 15~
77

~Chapter 16~
83

~Chapter 17~
90

~Chapter 18~
96

~Chapter 19~
100

~Chapter 20~
106

~Chapter 21~
110

~Chapter 22~
113

~Chapter 23~
121

~Chapter 24~
130

~Chapter 25~
136

~Chapter 26~
142

~Chapter 27~
149

~Chapter 28~
154

~Chapter 29~
161

~Chapter 30~

168

~Chapter 31~

172

~Chapter 32~

177

~Chapter 33~

183

~Chapter 34~

186

~Chapter 35~

195

A NOTE FROM THE AUTHOR - 207
ALSO BY TRIS WYNTERS - 209

CONTENT & TRIGGER WARNINGS

This book is a reverse harem/why choose. The female main character will have multiple love interests and will not have to choose between them.

This is a work of fiction that contains dark elements meant for mature readers only.

This book also discusses BDSM practices, which may make some readers uncomfortable. First and foremost, please note that consent is the main focus, as it should be.

A list of trigger warnings can be found on the next page. If you have additional questions or concerns, please reach out to triawyntersbooklover23@gmail.com.

Past Memories	***Present Story***
Coercion	Masked Men
Domestic Abuse	MM
Sexual Assault	MFM
Motorcycle accident	MMFMM
Suicidal ideation	DVP
Suicide by loved one	Coma
	Inability to bathe self
	Sedation
	CNC
	Primal Play
	Forced living arrangement
	Explosives
	Light Stalking
	Vigilante Shit
	Depression
	Panic Attacks
	Torture
	Flashbacks
	Inability to orgasm-
	Medical/Mental
	Murder

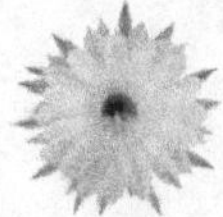

For those who want someone to fight for, just as badly as
you want someone to fight with.
Enjoy.
XOXO Tris

PLAYLIST

Under the Bridge by Red Hot Chili Peppers
Daylight by David Kushner
Edge of Desire by John Mayer
All I Want by Kodaline
Ronald by Falling in Reverse
Stay by Rihanna
Freak by Sub Urban
Daisy by Ashnikko
I Can't Help Myself (Sugar Pie, Honey Bunch)
by Four Tops
Birthday Cake by Rihanna
Little Girl Gone by CHINCHILLA
American Horror Show by SNOW WIFE
Take Me to Church by Hozier

TAG, WE'RE IT (A REVERSE HAREM DARK ROMANCE)

~CHAPTER 1~

Hands paw at my body; some rough and calloused, some smooth and firm, but they all paw nonetheless. Gripping, tweaking, flicking; my whole body tries to recoil from the intrusion.

Everything is dark. Too dark.

And, I can tell that I'm naked. Far too naked.

I flinch away from a hard squeeze of my breast, feeling as though it may burst in the man's hand. The pain is all-consuming until a heavy hand smacks my bare ass. I scream in agony, tears sliding down my cheeks like twin waterfalls.

"Shut up. No one cares about fat whores, Stupid girl." A deep voice sneers.

A big mitt of a hand wraps around my throat and squeezes, preventing any air from getting in or out. "You disgust me. You disgust us all."

The dark fabric covering my head is suddenly ripped away, and the inky darkness turns fuzzy.

Blinking my eyes a few times, I see that it's nighttime. We're in the woods behind my property; at the pile of limbs I had built up to burn.

I frantically look down and around me, my eyes slowly adjusting to the darkness as the moon reflects just enough light to make out my surroundings.

I'm in the burning pit I have for downed limbs, but it's different. The logs now form a wide circle around me instead of just being stacked randomly on top of each other. My feet are tied to the bottom of a giant root lying horizontally and cross-tied to a colossal limb that stretches far above my head. A quick tug confirms that my hands are roughly bound behind my back.

I also visually confirm that I am, in fact, completely and utterly naked. I force myself to stop crying even though my body shakes with humiliation and pain.

Movement to my right causes me to snap my gaze forward, and what I see almost immediately makes me puke as fear surges through my body.

Four men.

Four men, standing in front of the moonlight like death's children. They're all in black, standing calmly like they're waiting for my reaction. My eyes must be popping out of my skull as I take in their faces.

No, not faces...*masks.*

I try, and fail, to swallow multiple times as I look at each man.

One is tall and wide, like a football player. His dark clothes do nothing to tell me who he is or what he looks like, but his red Jason mask slashed with black markings is creepier than anything I've ever seen. The bright red of the mask looks all too much like blood. I'm usually not squeamish, but it's different when you're pretty sure *your* blood will be spilled next.

I shiver, and my bottom lip trembles. "P-p-please..." I beg, knowing it won't do any good. If these men plan to hurt me, they will, and there's nothing I can do about it.

The man next to "Jason" shifts his head as if assessing me. My eyes travel over him, and I take in the semi-realistic skull mask; or should I say, the top of one. The bottom part of the mask is just a few white lines slashed downwards, but the top of the skull mask, with the bottomless pits of eerie darkness in the place of eyes, causes me to stutter. I swear I can feel his eyes boring into mine; even though I can't see them. He's angry, yet cold...bloodthirsty.

"What's wrong, Baby girl? I thought you liked being scared?" The third man in line steps forward with his head cocked; a deep chuckle rumbling from behind his mask. His COD mask would generally turn me on, but tonight...tonight, all I feel is fear.

"W-why are you doing this to me?" The trembling in my body now seeps into my bones, like I'm being frozen from the inside out.

"You've been a bad girl. We know all about your nighttime activities. Who are you to play God? You're no better than they were." A sob rips out of my chest as I lower my head down, knowing this will be my end.

Fitting, really.

But it doesn't suck any less.

After another minute, the fourth and final man steps forward, his body almost close enough to touch mine. A single gloved finger lifts my chin until I grievously comply with the silent command. I nearly choke on a gasp as I come face-to-face with a Ghostface mask. The staccato sounds of his heavy breathing make me squirm with unease and impending doom.

His soft, gloved finger touches the side of my forehead before lazily trailing down my cheek, over my nose, and across my lips.

His fingertip taps my lips twice before stepping back and quietly tilting his head to the side.

I don't know how, but I swear I can feel his gaze trailing a path of fire and ice down my body.

Oh, so slowly, the man lifts his hand to the bottom of his mask. I vaguely realize the others are doing the same, but I'm riveted to the terrifying man before me.

The piercings, the cool blue eyes, the bright pink hair... "Stu?!"

So many emotions war within me, and I can't seem to land on one that fits.

"Your time has come, Beatrice," he says, sticking out his long tongue, and licking a trail up my neck. "Don't worry. We know how to make you scream."

Suddenly, he plunges a knife straight into my left leg, causing me to howl in pain; then immediately vomit all over the ground.

Male chuckles filter through the wooziness, and I lift my head in time to see the other three men step forward: Alpha, Even, and Danny.

All four men I've dreamed about; hopelessly wanted.

Then, there's Stu...

Moving my head to meet his gaze, I desperately implore, "Wh-why? Why are you doing this?"

His smirk is malicious, and my stomach sinks straight into my butt. "Did you really think we were friends? Oh, no." He mocks, turning his mouth down into an exaggerated pout.

He turns briefly toward the others before returning his glare to me. "We all knew who you were. It's our job to take down bad guys, remember? Well, in your case, bad *girl*. But hey... it worked out for us. We *all* got something out of it." His brows bounce up and down suggestively, but his eyes are full of malice.

He steps closer, whispering just against my ear, "And the best part is, you totally fell for us. Every. Single. One of us. It was far more fun than the usual way we tortured our targets. Wouldn't you say?" His brow raises as if he actually wants an answer.

However, I don't have time to respond. Instead, he stabs me straight in my right arm and slices it all the way down. The pain is far too much; too much physically, and far too much emotionally.

The shriek that comes from me echoes through the night just as a heavy fog sets in; stealing away my sight, my fear, my pain...

~CHAPTER 2~

Charlie

The bathroom door slammed shut only moments ago. Stu ran out of here like his ass had caught on fire. I'm torn between going after him and standing watch over Bea.

It takes me a few seconds before I realize that I'm holding the piece of paper Stu slammed into my chest before he left. It's none of my business, but I also need to know how to hel-

"Noooooo!!!! Aaaahhhhh!" Beatrice wails, her back nearly bowing off the bed.

I rush to her side, tossing the paper on the nightstand before sliding in beside her. Tears and sweat run down her face, soaking her nightdress.

Unfortunately, she's had quite a few of these night terrors. Doc says not to wake her, but we have to try to subdue her as quickly as possible to prevent her from hurting herself any further.

Scooting in the bed beside her, I try to remember what Stu did the last time, while also ensuring that I don't crush her casted leg.

Her breaths stutter repeatedly before a sob rips through the air; and my heart fucking shatters.

Reaching across her chest, including the tops of both arms, I curl my hand around her furthest bicep and pull her into me. Squeezing my eyes shut, matching the pain in my heart, I begin humming a tune under my breath. I press her against me while she thrashes wildly; crying, sniffling, whimpering.

After another moment of fighting to calm her, the lyrics to the tune I'm humming come to me. Not knowing what else to do, I start singing to her. I quickly realize that it was the first song I learned to play on the guitar. However, the understanding that I'm basically ripping my heart straight from my chest and offering it to her while she faces demons in her sleep has me stumbling over the lyrics.

Under the Bridge by the Red Hot Chili Peppers soothed my annihilated soul all those years ago; so it's fitting that it's returned to me once more.

Although my voice comes out raspy and broken, it appears to slowly penetrate through her night terror. Her sobs are turning into hiccups, and her body is beginning to settle.

Closing my eyes, I lift my hand away from her arm and slowly run my fingers through her sweaty hair, occasionally twirling a section for a moment before repeating the movement. Another whimper leaves her sweet lips, so I continue singing.

I break off as the air backs up in my lungs, the pain so close to the surface for me... and for Beatrice. *My little Omega.*

A soft, sweet snore pulls me out of my head long enough for me to realize that she's finally calm; finally resting. I slowly extract myself from Bea, leaning over to give her a brief peck against her temple before sliding off the bed.

For longer than necessary, I stare down at her, taking in every bruise, every scrape, every nose twitch...*everything.*

I did absolutely everything I could think of to prevent myself from falling for anyone again. Yet, here I am, desperately hoping Beatrice can forgive us, forgive *me,* and give us the chance to give her everything she deserves; to worship her the way she deserves.

With a frustrated growl under my breath, I roughly run my hand through my hair. The flickering of the letter Stu left behind catches my attention. Snapping it up, I lower my eyes long enough to see *her* name at the bottom. *What the fuck? She wrote him a letter? Why?*

A small voice in the back of my mind tells me it's none of my business. But a louder voice tells me I need to know so I can help him; help her.

As my eyes scan the written words, *her* words, I feel all of the air whoosh out of me. The rhythmic beating of the heart rate monitor is the only sound penetrating through the ringing of my ears.

My chest feels tight...far too tight. My heart crashes wildly against my ribcage, and I'm struggling to breathe. *Is this what a heart attack feels like?*

I briefly register the letter falling from my shaking hands. Hastily, I flee the room, rushing down the hallway. My world is hazy and unfocused, but I keep pushing. Those words- her words- *how could she? Why?*

Anger and fear rage in my heart as I break into a jog. My footsteps pounding against the floor seem to rattle the broken pieces of my heart.

Bursting through the back door, I fumble to take off my boots, then shuck off my clothes; stripping down to my boxers. I don't bother to check the temperature or check to see if there are clean towels in the storage cubby. I just dive right into our pool and begin kicking with all my might.

Three years... It's been three years since Cammy took her life. She was *mine*. Mine, *dammit*, and she ended her life like it was nothing. Like *I* was nothing. I knew she was struggling with things; things she would never talk to me, or anyone else, about.

She loved the scenes when we played together and was absolutely perfect as a sub. But her demons were too big. She wouldn't let me in. And six months after we met, she killed herself; in *my* bathroom while I was away on assignment. I couldn't take the grief, the disappointment, the knowledge that I wasn't good enough to help her. So, I sold the house a month later and moved in with the guys.

I breach the water's surface and inhale deeply before slicing through it in a freestyle stroke. The water sluices under my arms and whips past my body as I push myself to swim faster.

A year after Cammy died, Danny and Even started a relationship with another woman. I wanted nothing to do with her. Even thought I was being a prickly dick who needed a psychiatrist. But, deep down, I could sense that she was all wrong.

Unfortunately, three months after they made the relationship official, it all went to shit. Stu was in the middle of our annual finance audit and noticed some strange transactions. As it turns out, *Dana* was a little, thieving con artist.

And if that wasn't enough, her real name was Tanya, and she was on about a dozen different wanted lists worldwide. Thankfully, she never had access to our actual work files, so the only things that were compromised were Even and Danny's accounts. *Idiots.*

Last I heard, she had been extradited to somewhere overseas, where her punishment would be much more satisfying than she would have received here.

Hitting the far wall, I dip under the surface, flip, and turn before launching myself off the wall. My lungs begin to burn; frying off some of the emotions boiling inside of me.

Since Dana, none of us have dated. When we need to let off steam, we head to The Raven Room. Sometimes we play together, sometimes separately, and sometimes we just watch. But we don't play for keeps.

When I met Omega through a popular streaming app, I allowed myself to play into the fantasy with her; *of* her. She was perfect. So sweet, so gentle, yet so willing to be a good little submissive. Her responses rocked me harder than anyone else had in my life. And, dammit, that's fucking scary.

After her initial rejection, I gave up trying to hang out with her. I'm not too proud to back away and leave well enough alone. She didn't want anything more than what we had, and I respected that. But when I saw her in person and felt how deeply entwined she already was in my life, in *their* lives, I dared to dream.

Breaching the surface, I gasp for breath before damn near running into the wall; barely getting my arms up in time to slam them on top of the slate siding. My muscles ache and my lungs burn. But at least my emotions feel like they've been pushed into a corner far, far away.

I work on breathing, heaving, and panting as water drips from my hair to the ground. Closing my eyes, I see Bea's handwriting. She would have destroyed Stu. Sure, the rest of us would have been hurt, but none of us love her like he does. *Not yet.*

I push that thought away and focus on the issue: She was selfish and never stopped long enough to consider who she was leaving behind.

White hot rage courses through my body, and my jaw tenses to the point of pain. Never again. I will never let another person hurt me or my family again. As far as I'm concerned, it would be best if she were to heal and then disappear altogether. She's not a good fit for any of the guys. And the sooner they figure it out, the better. I don't care how hurt she is; once she's well enough to care for herself, she's out for good.

Liar.

CHAPTER 3

My skin prickles with awareness as a dark, heavy fog starts to lift off of me. My whole body aches; and I feel like I've been hit by a truck. *Oh! A truck!*

My eyes pop open and then immediately close again when the lights in the room burn my corneas. "Cheese and rice! Why is it so bright?" I grumble to myself.

"Because flowers need light to grow."

I scream out, well, sort of. My throat is dry and scratchy, and it feels like I tried to eat sandpaper. I try scrambling back into the bed, but my efforts are wasted. Instead, I cry out in pain from the pressure I put on my arms and legs.

Someone shushes me, the sound closer than before, as the most excruciating pain envelopes me. And I swear to all things holy; everything hurts, all the way to my bones.

"It's ok, Flower. Don't move. Doc said you can have more pain meds but he stopped administrating the sedative so you could wake up." His voice is warm, kind, and ridiculously sweet.

It's then that I feel wet cloth swipe across my forehead. I flinch back, pain coursing through me again. "It's ok, Flower. Don't move too much. You don't want your catheter ripped out. Believe me! It hurts." He cackles maniacally, and I frown, trying to figure out why that would be funny.

I keep my eyes closed as the man's voice moves around the room. I'm just so exhausted and in so much pain that I can't be bothered to care who it is. I assume it's a nurse since he said, "Doc," but whatever.

A cooling sensation fills my veins, and my head feels floaty again. *I like floaty. It's nice.*

"Just relax, Flower. I've got you." The low sound is sweet, sexy; like melted icing on a cinnamon roll. I like it.

"I like you, too, Flower." A low chuckle vibrates through his chest, and I feel myself smile as sweet, soft lips squish against my temple.

~CHAPTER 4~

My little flower drifts off to dreamland, and something warm and fuzzy fills me. She's so pretty. So perfect. So fucking cool.

She's a prickly little cactus- kind of like the picture she used on the kink app- but I don't shy away from pain. I quite like it, actually.

But, I know she's skittish, as well. I've promised Even that I would be on my best behavior so I don't scare her away. Still, I hate being away from her for long. Which, today, turns out to be a good thing. I waltzed in twenty minutes ago to check on her and found Stu nowhere in sight. I know Charlie is out back swimming, which is odd since it's 55°F outside. The water's gotta be way too cold; but to each his own.

I peer down at Beatrice, my precious flower, as I continue to swipe a cool, wet cloth across her forehead. Her nose scrunches adorably as she leans into the fabric and hums under her breath. That little noise causes my cock to stir, and our night at The

Raven Room replays through my mind. She was, and still is, utterly intoxicating. And *mine*.

A euphoric scent wafts through the room, and I smile as I continue my rhythmic strokes; cleaning off the sweat from Bea's face. "Hello, my Love. How was work?" I whisper, just loud enough for him to hear me. He was off doing recon on another target, so he's been gone most of the day.

I hear him shuffle into the room, a groaning sigh escaping him as he settles into the chair by the door. "Good. Fine. He'll be easy to take down. It only took him an hour to seek out Blaze. He left with a ridiculous amount of drugs. I almost took him then, but there were too many people around. He's got another meeting in a couple of days." He explains with a blasé tone, likely busy watching Bea and not really caring about the mission.

I nod, letting him know I've been listening, but don't comment. There's nothing to say, and honestly, I'm more than content watching Bea over the assholes we frequently track down.

We lapse into a comfortable silence as we watch over our sweet and sassy guest. *Well, not currently sassy, but she'll return to herself soon enough.*

After a few minutes, Even shuffles somewhere behind me. A crinkling of paper catches my attention, and I turn my head to look over at him over my shoulder. Even's bent over, reaching for something on the floor in front of him.

"What's that?" I inquire while resting my palm on top of Bea's tiny hand.

Even's face is pulled into a deep scowl as he sits up and straightens the crumpled paper. "I don't know. It was lying under the bed."

His eyes scan the paper back and forth quickly. I watch with rapt attention as his brows deepen, his eyes flash with pain and anger, and his usually tan skin lightens. He looks like he's going to be sick.

"Even, Love, what is it?" I implore, slipping from the bed and making my way to him. Squatting down in front of him, I rub my hands up and down his thighs, trying to coax him out of whatever trance he appears to be in.

The paper in his hand shakes lightly, and I can see the vein in his neck pulsing. "I. I can't..." He trails off, shaking his head in disbelief. Swallowing heavily, his eyes meet mine over the paper. Slowly, he tilts the page toward me, silently encouraging me to look at myself.

As I grab the paper, Even hoists me into his lap, my back against his chest, and nuzzles his face into my neck. It sets me on edge because he rarely seeks out comfort. He gives plenty of it when I or others need it, but he rarely searches it out for himself.

With a quick kiss to his forehead, I shift my head back to the paper in my hand. It takes me a while for the words to make sense. I have to read the letter three times before it becomes clear. Beatrice wrote a letter to Stu...saying goodbye...*forever*.

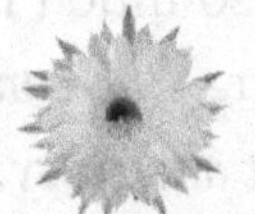 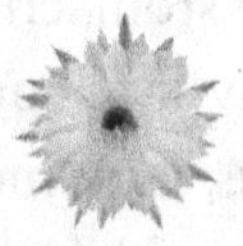

Dear Stu,

If you're reading this, I'm already gone. But don't
worry, I'm finally free.

You were the greatest light in my life when all I knew
was darkness. For that, I thank you. I know you won't
understand why I had to do this, but just know, I
probably would have done it much sooner had it not
been for you.

I'm sorry I got so mad at you. I was scared, exposed,
and felt all too vulnerable. So, I did what I do best; I
pushed you away no matter how much it hurt.

I want you to know, it wasn't you. I'm just too jacked
up. I did what I needed to do for me. I hope one day
you can forgive me.

Until then, know this: I love you, Stu; with every beat
of my crappy, dark, shattered heart. The thought of
living without you is so painful. But, having to live with
the memories of my past is unbearable.

I hope you find happiness, Stu. Even though I always
knew it wouldn't be with me. You deserve someone as
wonderful, kind, and awesome as you are. Never settle
for less.

Always and forever yours,

Beatrice

P.S. I know you live with your friends but, in case you
need more space, my lawyer should be contacting you
soon. My 10-acre property is all yours now. Enjoy it!

For me.

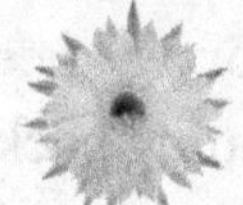

My stomach churns with anxiety and...rage. So much rage. I feel my face contort from pain-filled to menacing. *She can't just leave us; leave me. She's perfect and strong and smart and sassy. What was she thinking? Did something else happen? I mean, we stopped the last bastards from raping her, and she handled herself beautifully before then. Shit, who gouges out someone's eye in self-defense? She's a fucking badass! The world needs her.* I need her!

I turn and slide my hands onto Even's cheeks; his soft, full beard feels so good against my palms. I have to actively focus on *not* thinking about the dirty, dirty things I want to do to him.

His eyes are glassy, and I can tell he's moments away from letting the tears fall. With a soft kiss, I prod his firm, thick lips with mine before leaning back. "She didn't. She won't. She's here, and we'll help her; together."

Even's brows fold down, likely seeing how close my beast is lurking. His mouth opens, but-

Bam! The sound of the sliding glass door ricocheting in its tracks vibrates through the hall. I'm surprised it didn't shatter from the force. The sound of rushing and heavy footsteps distracts us from the letter still in my grasp.

Quietly, Even and I both lean over to peer out into the hallway in time to see a soaking-wet Charlie with a towel wrapped around his waist. His brows are drawn into his signature scowl, but I see something else reflecting in his eyes. I don't have time to question him as he tromps past the room without so much as a cursory glance.

Leaning back, Even and I share questioning looks.

Like we're of the same mind, we both scuttle to our feet and run out of the room. I don't make it three feet before I freeze; my feet unable to move as I take in the sight before me. Even barrels into me, grabbing me by my waist so I don't topple over. Our chests are heaving, and the sounds of our heavy breathing are the only sounds that I can hear as we watch Charlie's broad form squatting on the bathroom floor.

The growly rumble of his voice barely penetrates the silence as he begins whispering something. The perfect sculpted muscles in his back, shoulder, and arms twitch and flinch as he leans forward. With a low grunt, he moves to stand.

Even and I watch as Charlie slowly and meticulously adjusts something near the crook of his arm before he turns sideways to move out of the bathroom. That's when we see the pink mop of hair.

He knows. Poor fucking Stu knows.

When Charlie squeezes his large frame through the door, Even and I immediately jump into action. Stu's either passed out or entirely out of it. Either way, he needs to be in bed. Even turns and heads down the hallway in front of Charlie and leads the charge upstairs to Stu's room. I bring up the rear, beelining into the kitchen for a bottle of water, before meeting them in Stu's room.

When I walk in, Stu's eyes are closed, but it's obvious how swollen they are. His face is red and clammy, and there seems to be an imprint on the side of his face; from the bathtub ledge, by the looks of it.

Glancing up, I look at Charlie to figure out if he knows. It would explain the pool laps and how he seemed to know precisely where Stu was; knowing he needed help. But, he has the best, blank face I've ever seen. Although, his eyes are almost unfocused as he stares at Stu's form.

His body, on the other hand, tells a different story. His fists clench, unclench, clench, unclench. The muscles in his pecs and arms ripple with every movement, and his jaw bulges from the sides, where he squeezes it shut. *Fuck... if he read the note...Cammy.*

My eyes go wide as I try to subtly get Even's attention. He must feel my gaze on him as he quickly snaps his head from watching over Stu to pinging his eyes between mine. I see it the moment he puts it together. His confused frown forms into fear, and his skin becomes pale. His head quickly whips over to Charlie; likely scanning him the way I did, searching for any clues that Charlie has read the letter.

Charlie sucks in a deep breath, closes his eyes, and releases it before stomping back out of the room. His door kicking shut echoes down the hall, leaving Even and I cloaked in silence.

Well, shit, this just keeps getting worse, but one thing's for sure: Our little family is falling apart, and it's up to Even and I to keep us together.

~CHAPTER 5~

Awareness prickles the edge of my consciousness. I don't like it. I want to go back to the quiet, floaty feeling. But... I'm already starting to shift uncomfortably.

Memories, nightmares, sounds, and images begin flashing through my mind, and I whimper out. I have no idea what's real and what's my imagination, but the pain, the pain in my heart, is so very real.

"It's okay, Little Flower. I'm here. You're okay." The voice is so familiar; comforting. I wonder if it's a memory or another nightmare.

"Neither." A delicious chuckle rolls over my body and causes it to tingle. "I'm here with you, silly girl. I'm real. You're real. And you're okay."

Oh shoot, I must have said that out loud.

With much more effort than should be necessary, I flutter my eyes open. The light isn't obscenely bright, like the last time I was in the hospital, but it still burns. Squeezing them closed for a moment, I take a deep breath. Well, I try to, but pain spiders through my chest and stomach, causing me to groan embarrassingly loud.

"Careful, Flower. You have a long road of recovery ahead of you. But, don't worry, I'll be here every step of the way."

Normal people would be relieved by someone wanting to take care of them. I never claimed to be normal.

My eyes pop open, blinking away the haze as I take in my surroundings and, most importantly, the man in the room with me.

Panic immediately sets my heart racing as I realize I'm definitely *not* in a hospital room. I'm in a bedroom, a beautiful one. Not stuffy, but not dull, either.

It's pretty perfect, actually.

Looking down, I see I'm in a large, comfortable forking bed. I can feel myself scowl with confusion as I realize that my favorite weighted blanket is sprawled across me. *How the heck?*

Looking to my left, I gaze through the far window, gawking at a gorgeous, shimmering pool; a single, white diving board sitting on the far edge. And I do mean *far*. It's absolutely massive, and I briefly wonder if it's Olympic-sized. But then, I remember that I still need to figure out where I am.

Turning my attention back to the room, I admire how the navy blue chaise lounge is perfectly positioned next to the window. Scanning the wall, I find myself smiling at the light gray painted walls, the top six inches adorned with white decorative swirls.

It's simple, yet beautiful.

I vaguely remember a small nightstand with a bottle of water to my left and a charcoal gray, tufted armchair sitting on the wall across from me, right next to the door. But I immediately forget all of that the moment I see *him* standing there. A huge grin spreads across his face, and his maple eyes shine excitedly.

Dark stubble covers his face's bottom half, and his shaggy black hair is tousled and unruly. My eyes briefly dip down to see that he's wearing dark blue jeans, a heather red V-neck shirt, and he's barefoot. *Why is that hot?*

A deep chuckle snaps me out of my perusal and immediately causes me to blush deeply. My gaze flies to his, and I scowl indignantly. "Something funny?" I swear I try to sound angry and irritated, but it's hard to be taken seriously when there's a whole forking desert in my mouth.

His face falls, and his eyes widen with alarm. He rushes to my side, causing me to flinch away. Thankfully, he slows his movements as he steadily offers me a bottle of water with a straw sticking out; his brows pinched with worry.

My gaze pings between him and the bottle before self-preservation wins out. I legitimately feel like I'm dying from thirst.

Leaning forward, I lock my gaze on his as I slowly shift over to him, grunting and tensing with pain, before taking the straw in my mouth and sucking down half the bottle. I swear to all things holy, it's like drinking from the fountain of life. It simultaneously quenches a bone-deep need, cools me off, and rouses me back to life.

Releasing the straw, I suck in a few breaths. Sighing heavily, I close my eyes and lean back against the headboard of what I can confidently say is the comfiest bed I've ever been on.

I hear the bottle crinkle a little before it's placed on the nightstand to my right.

Keeping my eyes closed, I pointedly block out the fact that the room is engulfed in silence; which means he's just sitting, or standing, there. I don't know.

Taking a few controlled breaths, I begin taking stock of my body and try to piece together what happened, as opposed to why the heck I'm in a bedroom and not a hospital.

There are a few odd sensations: pain in my chest, itching pain down my left side, and two *heavy*, hard-feeling bandages on one arm and one leg.

Curiosity finally wins out, and I slowly open my eyes. I move my right arm first, knowing it feels uncomfortably heavy, and it takes me an embarrassingly long time to process the fact that there's a deep blue cast. Twisting and turning it, I slowly move my fingers until a spark of pain shoots down my arm. A tiny yelp escapes me, and I have to blink back the tears and fight off the swirl of nausea threatening to take me under.

"Easy, Flower." His voice is so close. Then, I feel his soft hands start running down my hair.

Flinching away, I allow anger to override my fear, my pain, my confusion. "What am I doing here, Danny?" I spit, my eyes snapping open to meet his annoyingly sweet gaze.

We stare at each other, his grin widening with each passing second while my scowl deepens. I feel him lean in closer, inhaling deeply before brushing a chaste kiss to the top of my head.

I growl, or try to since my throat is still dry, and move my left arm to help me fling off the blanket. I instantly regret twisting my body and struggle through gritted teeth to lift the monstrosity that is my weighted blanket.

"Beatrice. Stop. Let me help you." Danny whispers, sounding so sweet and sincere that I choke on a sob.

"No! I don't need your help!" I absolutely realize that I sound like a petulant child, but at this point, the rational side of my brain is clearly not working.

Danny completely ignores me, choosing to whip the blanket off of my body instead. The visual immediately makes me want to pull the covers right back up.

My left leg is in a black cast that starts from about mid-thigh and wraps all the way down, covering everything but my swollen little toes. My right leg is swollen and completely scratched up, as if I got into a fight with a pack of cats.

My perusal ends when I meet the edge of a black nightgown. Tilting my head further down, I see that it's actually one of mine. It's one of my favorite tank dresses that I got from Beautiful Disaster. The front is lilac swirls surrounding the words Beautiful Disaster, and there is a little fairy with lilac hair and white wings reading a book. The back of the dress is racerback style, with the same fairy from the front sitting at the top in the center, happily reading her book. Below is a trail of lilac swirls before the words, "And she lived...Authentically Ever After".

It feels soft and comforting, and I have to close my eyes to push back the tears threatening to spill over. Sucking in a few deep breaths, I will myself to get it together.

My body trembles as emotions flood through me. Danny's soft, warm hands snake behind my back, against the headboard, and I feel his body subtly shift onto the bed. He nuzzles into me while gently squeezing me; apparently aware of more bruises than I am at this point.

He starts saying random words; judging by his tone, they're meant to be comforting. But I can't process them. My heart is beating in my ears, and someone's loud sobs echo through the room.

Danny doesn't move. He appears completely nonplussed about the sound, about the fact that a basic stranger is falling apart in his arms. Danny just brushes his hand down my shoulder, leaning his head against mine, as the sensations, the pain, and the emotions completely overtake me like a tidal wave.

Eventually, the screaming dies down- embarrassingly cueing me in that the sound was coming from me- and my tears begin to dry up. My eyes are heavy, and my body just *forking* hurts.

Somewhere...somewhere deep in the recesses of my mind, I hear Danny quietly singing. It takes me a moment to place the lyrics of Daylight by David Kushner. It's haunting, soothing, and I briefly wonder if there's a reason he chose it.

Regardless, it becomes the perfect lullaby for me to drift off to.

~CHAPTER 6~

A gentle knock rouses me from sleep. It takes me a couple of minutes to push out of my sleep-addled brain and look around. Danny is gone, the side of the bed he was lying on is now cold, and I find myself frowning.

Another knock pulls me from my strange reaction, and I shake my head, hoping to clear it a little more. "C-Come in," I weakly call out. I still have no idea where I am. I'm injured, and it's not like I can defend myself, so my heart rate doubles as the door swings open.

But, the reassuring smile from the man before me makes me feel instantly at ease.

"Hi, Doc." I last met Doc after the guys saved me from a meet-up gone wrong. He patched me up while I was in a dissociative state. Thankfully, he also left his information to reach out if I had questions or wanted a rape kit conducted. A few days later, I made the decision to call. His voice on the phone was soothing, almost paternal, and I was oddly comforted by his demeanor. I agreed to meet with him for a slew of tests, needing to make sure I didn't get anything from the jerks I encountered that night. While I was *pretty sure* the one guy didn't get a chance to insert anything more than his fingers, there was a lot of bloodshed that night. And, a girl can never be too careful.

Doc's wide smile instantly puts me at ease, and I try scooting to sit up in bed. With a long hiss of pain, and a lot of inching like a fat caterpillar, I finally get into a comfortable position, leaning up against the headboard.

"How are you doing, young lady?" I playfully scoff at his identifier, rolling my eyes heavenward.

"I'm fine, Doc. We really should stop meeting like this." I give him a self-deprecating smile and try to shrug a shoulder, although that ends with me wincing in pain.

"Easy, there," He admonishes me, stepping forward. He removes the stethoscope from his neck and asks permission to check me over.

Fifteen minutes later, I've been poked, prodded, and seen every scratch, burn, and cut along my body. I am utterly worn out. Thankfully, I had my catheter removed, as well.

Doc's just finishing with the instructions for my medication regimen and plans to meet at his clinic in a few weeks to scan my arm and leg to make sure they're healing properly.

Turning towards me, he silently assesses me. I squirm under his gaze, fiddling with my fingers in my lap.

When the silence becomes too much, I blurt out, "Where am I? And why am I *here*?"

He gives me a gentle smile and inhales deeply. I'm already bracing myself for his answer, knowing it's not going to be as cut and dry as what I want. "The guys are very protective of those they care for. Bringing you here; they can help you heal and recover."

I feel the V between my brows deepen as I tilt my head. I'm not even sure which part of that I'm more confused about.

Doc doesn't give me an opportunity to figure it out before he adds, "You'll have to ask them for more information, but you must be something special for them to bring you here. Besides, given the opposing arm and leg casts, you will need a lot of help. Anyway, I must get going. If you need anything, the guys can ring."

He wraps a hand around the now unplugged heart monitor and begins rolling it toward the door.

Just when I think he's going to walk right out and leave me alone in a place with near strangers, he suddenly stops in the doorway. Turning his head back towards me, he sighs heavily and draws his brows together, like he's nervous about something. "I know they don't always show it, but they're good guys. And, once they bring someone in, they move heaven and hell to protect them. Just remember that before you rip their balls off." He smirks like he's imagining it before winking.

Then, he turns from the door and disappears.

Male voices carry through the house, causing goosebumps to break out all over my body. *I remember Danny being here earlier. Does that mean I'm in their house? With all of them? How did I even get here?*

Unfortunately, I don't have time to overthink it; yet. The last dose of meds Doc gave me are slithering their way through my system, and my eyes are becoming heavy.

With a few whimpers and groans, I finally relax into the bed and let sleep claim me.

CHAPTER 7

About an hour ago, after a swift reprimand and a knowing look, Doc left us. The bastard is too perceptive for his own good. Thankfully, he told us that Bea is doing well, all things considered, and should be ready to start slowly moving around. Unfortunately, one of us is going to have to help bathe her when she's ready, and I just know she's going to hate that.

Stu has basically been mute since he emerged from his room almost 18 hours after Charlie tucked him in. He stood, looking forlorn as hell, as Doc filled us in. I don't even think he's been back in Bea's room since the letter. I know Charlie hasn't. Not that I blame him, after what happened to Cammy.

Danny said he had someone in the basement who he needed to finish interrogating, so I offered to stay with Bea. I've been sitting in this big-ass armchair, listening to her sweet snores and occasional whimpers, while writing random shit on my tablet. My ass is starting to go numb, but until one of the others comes in, I'm not going to leave. Heaven forbid she tries to go to the bathroom by herself.

And she would. *Stubborn ass woman.*

I'm just starting to pen another line when Bea gasps suddenly. My head snaps up toward her in time to see her squeeze her eyes closed as she sucks in a breath. She's almost sitting up completely while cradling the arm in a cast.

I slip out of my chair, sliding my tablet onto it, and slowly step towards her with my hands up. "Careful, Bea. It's going to be ok. Just take it easy. What can I get you?" My voice starts firm and cautious, but the way my voice quivered at the end gives my anxiety away.

Her head snaps up to mine, and a sea of emotions passes through her eyes before she finally settles on irritation. I can practically feel her displeasure radiating off of her, but I keep inching forward like a stupid, stupid man.

"I'm just here to help, Bea." I resign, lowering my hands as I get close enough to see that she's shifting from irritation to pure anger.

"Why? Why am I here, Even?" She spits out my name and scrunches her nose like it smells bad. I take a few breaths, trying to gather my thoughts as the sassy, sexy, blue-eyed woman in front of me seems to be returning back to her wonderful self. It fills me with a sense of pride. Letters and intentions aside, she's so much stronger than she gives herself credit for.

"Even!" She barks, startling me from my thoughts and effectively wiping the small grin off my face. "Y-yes. Sorry." I respond almost sheepishly before getting my shit together. "Listen, we care about you whether you like it or not. You need help, help we can provi-"

"That's what hospitals are for E! Why am I *here*? Where the fork *is* here?" She exhales roughly through her nose; like a cute little bull. I have to work to suppress a smile. This woman drives me crazy.

Clearing my throat, I take another step closer to her. "Beatrice," I start in a low voice. "You were alone. Always alone. The doctors needed to make sure someone could be around to help. Thankfully, you have four men who are crazy about you, willing to help, willing to do anything necessary to get you back on your feet, to help you get stronger, to take care of you."

Her head has been shaking back and forth, trying to negate what I'm saying, and fresh tears are streaming down her face. She's no longer looking at me, but I continue on.

"We wanted you to be safe, with one of us with you at all times, until you recover. So, we brought you to our house after Doc cleared it with the hospital. We had to wait a couple of days for your body to be healed enough for transport. And, trust: Doc would not have let us bring you here unless he was absolutely sure he could take care of you, and he trusted us to do the same. So, um, you've been here a couple of days. In our home."

I don't mean to ramble on, but I'm afraid. Afraid she's going to *what? Get up and run out of here? I don't know...but I need her to be comfortable.*

"We gave you the room on the bottom floor because it has the best view and, when you start walking, you won't need to take the stairs. The bathroom is just two doors down, and you can easily access the kitchen. Not that you need the kitchen; we can get you anything you want. But, um, the bathroom..." I choke out a cough and palm my neck, strangely uncomfortable. *This is so not like me. Snap out of it, E.*

I feel her eyes on me as she squeaks out, "Bathroom?"

The non-question question hangs in the air. I glance at her in time to see her eyes widen and her face pale. "Oh my God! No, no. I'm ok. I've got it. You've done enough. I can go home now."

She moves like she's going to stand, yanking the lone IV out of her hand and shifting toward the side of the bed. I can tell she's clenching her teeth, and sweat starts to bead on her forehead.

"Beatrice, please. Beatrice, stop!" She shakes her head dismissively as she tries to stand. Caution turns into desperation as visions of her falling and hurting herself flicker through my mind.

Basically towering over her, I look down, physically blocking her from standing, as she starts to beat on me with her free arm.

"Move, Even!" She snarls. "Get out of my way!"

"No! You stubborn ass woman. Lie the fuck down, now!" I don't mean to snap or yell, but dammit, she's going to hurt herself more.

Thankfully, the little submissive still deep inside of her obeys immediately. Her movements halt, and she gapes at me, her eyes wide with indignation. At herself or with me, I'm not sure. But hey, at least she stopped moving.

"Good. Now, listen up and listen good: You have a cast on your arm and a cast on your opposite leg. You have severe road rash along with a dozen other scrapes, burns, and cuts. You are *not* leaving this house until you are well and truly healed. You *will* get help moving to and from the bathroom, you *will* ask for help when the pain is too much, and you will *not* argue with us. We care, whether you like it or not, and we want you to get better. Even if that means that you leave this house at the end of six weeks and never speak to us again. Got it?"

Her eyes are round and doe-like, and I momentarily have to remind myself that it's not the best time to get hard.

Silence hangs in the air as neither of us moves. We are both frozen, me still slightly towering over her and her still sitting partially off the bed. Our breaths are the only thing that you can hear in the room now that Doc has taken away the heart monitor.

After far too long of our stilted breaths mingling in the quiet, tears burn down her face. *And I do mean burn.* Her eyes fill with so much vitriol that it cracks my heart in two. "Whatever," she spits in disdain. "You've been a good little lap dog. You can leave now." She turns away, sliding into the bed while biting her lip to cover the sounds of her pain while trying to turn over.

Part of me wants to leave. I want her to want me and I don't want to hurt her or brush off her discomfort. But, her stubbornness is one of the things I love best about her. And, I know she really does need us right now.

"Bea, I will leave. I will sit in the chair outside the door, but before I do, I need to know," she stops shifting uncomfortably, signaling that she's at least listening.

When I don't get anything else from her, I blow out a breath, rubbing my hand through my too-long beard, then clench my fists. "Do you have to go to the bathroom?"

Her body tightens suddenly. I would have missed it if I hadn't been staring down at her. "No." Her voice is quiet, pained, but her body language tells me differently.

"Dammit, woman! Do you really hate me so much that you're willing to get a UTI just to prove you don't need help? Jesus, Beatrice!" I'm wobbling on a tightrope of emotion.

Stepping back, I run my hands through my hair, growling under my breath and pulling enough that my scalp prickles.

I don't know how long I pace, wrapped up in the torrent of my own emotions, but I'm panting and sweaty by the time her sweet-as-fuck voice breaks through the tension in my body. "Fine." It's quiet and filled with disdain, but it's a start.

Whirling around, I face her and take a deep breath. Once the fizzle in my body fades, I step towards her and nod once; my face completely serious and void of the raging emotions warring inside of me. "OK." My voice is gruff, clipped, but it's all I can get out without letting the rest of my emotions out.

With a trembling nod, and another tear leaking from her eye, she slowly rolls back towards me and lifts her casted arm. As gently as possible, I scoop her into my arms, ensuring that I bring the nightgown down near her knees so I keep her modesty.

Her hisses and lurches of pain break my heart, but as I knew she would, she grits through it. I gingerly make my way through the room, diligently maneuvering her through the doorway and walking her to the bathroom.

Once there, however, I feel torn. I don't want to hurt her, but I don't want to just leave her here, either.

"Can you, um. Can you set me down now?" Her voice is low, unsure, and it causes me to smile down at her. Her eyes are glassy but still so damn beautiful, and I feel myself stumble on a breath.

Finally, I squat down, oh so slowly, until her feet hit the floor. Her body starts shivering violently as she tries to shift some of the weight from me to her own legs. Her arms stay firmly wrapped around my neck while mine move to her right hip and her back. I try to avoid the road rash streaking down her left side.

For at least a full minute, we stay in that position. Her tremors don't subside, but I feel her slowly starting to remove one arm. "Ready?" I ask her quietly.

Her hand flexes on my shoulder, and I hear her swallow audibly. "Y-y-yes."

With a gentle nod, I keep my hands anchored to her waist as I steadily stand from my squatting position. As I rise, her arms slowly slip away, and she slowly shifts, allowing her body to be positioned in front of the counter so she can use it for support.

As soon as she's standing, mostly on her own, I lean down and whisper. "Got it?"

She nods weakly and releases a shaky breath. Gradually, I relax the hold I have on her, only taking a step back when I am sure she's mostly stable.

I lean over and flip the lid of the toilet next to the sink before straightening again. I meet her gaze in the mirror and can't help the smile that moves across my face. My brave, fierce, badass woman is standing proudly on her own just days after a horrific motorcycle crash. *She truly is amazing.*

"You can leave now." She speaks under her breath, breaking eye contact and eyeing the toilet like it's an alligator lying in wait. I don't look away, hoping she'll meet my gaze again, but alas, she doesn't.

With a final nod, I move out of the bathroom, clasping onto the handle to close the door behind me.

"This doesn't change anything. I will never forgive you. Any of you." Her whispered words trail off at the end of her statement; as if the thought of what we did causes her more pain than her injuries.

I don't respond. I just close the door and wait until she calls for me to help her back to bed.

Forcing her to move here will either prove to be the best idea ever... or the worst.

~CHAPTER 8~

Trying to use the bathroom when your entire body feels like it's been run over by a truck- *or thrown off a motorcycle-* is ridiculously difficult. My whole body shakes, and everything radiates pain. I hiss out when the back of my thighs hit the cold porcelain, tensing momentarily before releasing a deep breath and slumping forward.

After I do my business, which feels darn near orgasmic for some reason, I clean myself, flush, then use the counter to lift myself. I don't know what is more awkward, the cast on my dominant hand or the giant leg cast. It all feels heavy and weird and makes me shutter with discomfort.

When I finally make it upright, sort of, I shimmy my panties up my thighs and over my rear. It's excruciating and, honestly, super annoying that it takes so long.

I continue using the counter to bear most of my weight as I edge along the vanity, stopping when I'm positioned in front of the simple mirror. I take a moment to catalog the bruising and cuts all around my neck, chest, and down my arms.

It's unsightly at best. *I'm* unsightly at best.

My body begins to quake more violently and I can feel my eyes beginning to droop. Pushing through, I reach out a trembling hand to turn on the water so I can wash my hands. "Forkin' nut balls," I mutter, realizing that I basically only have the tops of four fingers on my right hand to help me wash.

"You ok in there, Baby Girl?" I jump with a yelp, having forgotten Even was out there.

"I'm fine! And don't call me that." I lash out. For one: He startled me. And two: I don't want his sweet words. He betrayed me, lied to me, tricked me.

He may be helping me right now, but I'm not falling for his crap again.

Even doesn't respond as I continue trying to clean my hand, and fingers, before rinsing. Leaning over, I grab the navy towel hanging on the cloth ring and dry off.

A deep voice causes goosebumps to scatter across my arms. I'm unsure who it belongs to, but I know it's not Even. He also sounds far away enough that I can't make out all the words. "...doing out here?"

"She had to go to the bathroom." Now, that was Even.

"...babysitter. Remember the deal... only until she heals." Something familiar prickles at the edge of my memory, and I think it may be Alpha. *Or whatever his real name is.*

One thing's for sure: he is not happy about me being here. *Yeah, well, that makes two of us, buddy.*

Even's response seems quieter, but I can still hear the blatant disgust in his tone. "Don't fucking start. You care just as much as we do. Don't take out your feelings from the past on her."

That's it. I'm done.

I fling the door open, tears rising in my eyes as pain bursts through my body from the movement. "I'm not happy about being here either, *Alpha.* I didn't ask to be here. *You* don't want me here. So, here's a novel idea: take me home!" My voice rises with each passing word, and I know my deep scowl mirrors his.

He looks like he's about to burst into flames, even as his eyes scrutinize my body. I try crossing my arms to appear like the fighter I pretend to be, but the awkward way I hold my cast just makes me look stupid. I know this, and judging by the glint in his eyes, he does, too.

"Listen," He snarls, stepping closer to where Even and I are standing, "You are here because you need help getting better. You, *little girl-*" he spits the term like it's a curse word. Maybe it is. "Were all *alone. You* can't recover on your own. So deal with it. Just don't come crying to me if you need anything. You have the other three tripping over their dicks for you, and I want no part in it."

The pure venom in his words causes a flush of bright, red anger to burn across my body. I tense my jaw before taking a deep breath. "Fine. By. Me," I harshly grit before stepping into the hall.

My heart rate is sky-high, and I hear a high-pitched ringing in my ears. But I push through.

I'm not going to be asking any of these jerks for help.

Too bad my body wasn't on board. But, the moment I shove past his huge frame, having to slide sideways against the wall, my world tilts.

Then, I'm enveloped by darkness.

~CHAPTER 9~

Charlie

I let my anger cloud my judgment. I should have seen the signs. They were so damn obvious. Her skin, usually creamy and slightly pink, was damn-near cadaverous. Her eyes were red-rimmed and puffy, and her whole body was shaking; *and not in a sexy way.*

I was trying to intimidate her, trying to make her submit to my anger, so I almost missed it. I almost missed her as she fell face-first towards the ground. I barely managed to fling my arm around her mid-section before she gained another bruise. Thankfully, it was easy enough to twist a little and scoop her into my arms.

Now, I'm standing here with this damn woman in my arms, and I can't move. I can't fucking move. I'm just stuck, staring down at her limp, broken form. It's not lost on me that the last time I touched her like this was the night of the accident. The night we almost lost her. The night before she planned to kill herself.

"

Anger roars through my veins as that recollection buries itself deep in my bones; like a cancer eating away at me.

"Charlie..." Even's low voice pulls me out of my mind long enough to get me moving. I flee with her to the guest room, Even's heavy footsteps trailing behind me. I make it to her bed and have to force myself not to toss her on it. I can't take it. I can't take her body touching mine. I can't take the sight of her looking so God damn broken.

Once she's placed on the bed, I turn so abruptly that I bump into Even. "Woah. You ok, man?" He steadies me with his hand on my shoulder before ripping it away. His eyes widen as he takes in my face, his eyes darting between mine.

Awareness trickles in, and I focus on "fixing my face," as Stu calls it. With a nod, and a sort of grunt, I run from the room.

Today is uncharacteristically cool for November near Houston, Texas, so I don't bother with swimming. Instead, I head up the stairs toward my room, slamming the door the moment I cross the threshold.

I roughly rub my hands back and forth across my head, letting the pain from the friction ground me. Pacing the room, I consciously pack up all the bullshit, all the feelings I thought I had for Omega- *Beatrice*- and pack them in a tiny little box.

A growl of irritation rumbles up through my chest, and I pound over to my maroon La-Z-Boy on the opposite side of the room. I slam my body into it, forcing the air from my lungs. My heart feels like it's in my throat, and I hate everything about this situation. I feel out of control, lost, and just plain crazy. This woman has us all fucked up.

Needing to release some tension before returning to our current job, I pick my guitar off the stand to my left, slide the pick from its spot between the fretboard and the strings, and close my eyes. Absent-mindedly, I start moving my fingers along the strings, plucking them at just the right time. I let my thoughts go as my feelings drain out of my hands and into the chords playing through the room. Once I hit the chorus, I scoff at myself and roll my eyes. Of course, my brain would decide to play John Mayer's Edge of Desire.

My heart squeezes, but I don't let it take me over. Instead, I lose myself to the notes surrounding me, allowing them to soothe something so deep inside me that I'm not sure I ever want to stop.

I drowned myself in music for over an hour. The pads of my fingers hurt in the best way, and I feel clearer; more myself. After making another pot of coffee, I swiped a protein bar and am now staring at the maps of our area and the three cities bordering ours.

We can't pin down these damn Crimson Knights, and they're starting to interrupt the local businesses. They're pushing past drug running and are just being absolute dicks.

Like, why go to Mr. Napoli's and destroy the pizzeria his father opened a year before cancer took him away?

And Craving Kernels: nicest damn people you'll ever meet and the best, and strangest, flavors you could ever think of. For some reason, a bunch of the knights snuck in and set off enough fireworks to consider it a July 4th celebration. The business had to completely shut down; indefinitely.

Hell, last week, two of them purposefully crashed Hummers into stop-light poles, effectively screwing up two major streets in town right at the start of rush hour. *Fucking asswads.*

I slam my hands on the desk as I try to find a pattern, a central point, *any-fucking-thing.*

The biggest problem with the Crimson Knights is that they aren't easily identifiable. There are no "colors," no "tats," nothing that makes them stand out in any way.

In fact, the only reason we know who to thank for the bullshit is because of the little insignias they leave behind. It reminds me of those pressed penny machines at the zoo or museums; the elongated oval, thin, zinc and copper object stretched to its limit. When holding the token vertically, you can see the image of a knight stamped in the middle. Slightly curved, vertically, around each side are the words "Crimson"- on the left- and "Knights"- on the right.

It's stupid, and cheap, and shitty, and I fucking hate them.

We find one of these little pennies at almost every damn location where something ridiculous happens. It's like these assholes are you trying to find the most bizarre ways to fuck up others' lives.

Scrubbing a hand down my head, I lean back in my chair and begin rocking. Tapping my pen against my mouth, I try to find a different angle to work from. There's something we're missing.

A knock on the door pulls my attention from the giant Christmas light knot of information tangled in my brain. "Yeah," I call out.

The door opens, and Stu pokes his head in. He looks like absolute shit. I feel myself scowl as anger coils through my body. *Fucking Beatrice.*

"Hey, Boss. I got a call from HQ. They want us to take on another job. I sent the info through email. It should be easy enough. I'm going to stake it out tonight. Probably can take 'em tomorrow or the day after." His voice is quiet, all business, and completely void of his usual sunny disposition.

I nod my head in understanding and take a deep breath as my mind switches gears from one target to another. Shaking the mouse next to my computer, I enter my password and navigate to our hidden email server.

As it loads the information, I look back at Stu, and my heart pinches a little. I've always been protective of Stu. Yes, I'm protective of all the guys, but Stu... I don't know. It's just different. He's like a goofy little brother.

To see him so off, so fucking miserable, makes me want to burn the world down. Hell, it makes me want to hug him. Which is fucking weird because I barely handle touch. However, over the last year or so, he's randomly patted my shoulder or arm or used them for support, and I haven't flinched away.

Either way, I need to figure out how to bring that wide grin and those crazy dimples back. I need Stu back.

He stands quietly in the doorway as I scan the information he already tracked down. He's right; this should be relatively easy. This douche has been using his status as a revered motivational speaker and sex therapist to take advantage of young women reaching out for help. The scumbag takes their money to "invest," promises them the world, uses the guise of BDSM to do whatever they want in bed, no safeword allowed, and then drops them; acts like he has no idea who they are. The sneaky bastard even deposited the checks under an umbrella corporation that's not linked to his name.

Unless, of course, you have a Stu.

Glancing back at him, I nod and take a deep breath. "I'll go with you. I need to get the fuck outta here. We could use an easy case."

A yawn slips out at the end and Stu chortles. "You need a nap first, Boss Man?" Rolling my eyes, I crumple up a paper and toss it at his head. He dances out of the way, and a slight smile tips his mouth. *There he is.*

"Let the others know we're leaving tonight. They can babysit the little girl." I sneer at the thought of her. A miserable mixture of lust and irritation descends on me, and I forcefully shake my head, hoping to erase it like an etch-a-sketch.

I realize Stu hasn't left yet, so I glance back at him and almost kick my own ass. He's pale again, his eyes are watery and glossed over, and he looks like he's moments from curling in a ball and checking out.

With a rough exhale, I scrub my face, feeling the prickles under my palms, and look back at him. "Stu, I'm sorry. I just-" I heave a sigh, then groan in frustration. "Forget her. You're too good for her, and you don't deserve anything she's done to you. Once she's all healed, we'll all get back to normal; she'll be out of our lives, and we won't have to be shit on for simply helping. We did nothing wrong." My voice has turned angry, and I'm pretty sure I growled.

Stu nods, barely mumbles, "Yeah," and turns away, closing the door behind him. I know that wasn't the right thing to say. I do. The problem is: I'm not just pissed, I'm fucking hurt.

And that is so much worse.

The fog of sleep hangs heavy in my mind, and I groan out. Shifting in the bed with my eyes still closed, I burrow deeper into the safety and comfort of my weighted blanket. Of course, the comfort doesn't last long as I hear something that sounds an awful lot like a page being turned.

Popping my eyes open, my heart rate spikes as I take in everything around me. Realization finally settles as I remember I am *not* at home. I'm at the guys' house, and someone is in the room with me.

My brows furrow as I scan the room. The door is partially open, but I don't see anyone there. Someone must have moved the chair outside because it's now missing from its spot next to the door. The chaise is free of any unfairly sexy men, and I question if maybe I've lost my sanity. I swore I heard-

Another page flip echoes in the otherwise quiet room. Now that I'm a little more awake, I realize it's coming from the floor beside me.

Biting my lip to keep all the painful noises from erupting, I scooch closer to the right side of the bed, careful not to twist my casted arm and peer down.

A mop of crazy, wavy black hair greets me, and I find myself grinning. From my view above him, I can see he's leaning against the side of the bed, his knees bent as he reads a book. I don't know what it is, but I can't help but watch him for a moment. Like, I'm getting to see something most people don't.

He huffs out a sound in response to something he read, and I have to suppress the giggle that wants to bubble out. *Why the heck is he so dang adorable?*

He shifts to turn the page again, and my arm freezes mid-air.

Realizing I was unconsciously moving to run my fingers through his hair, I whip it back to the bed. That would have been far too intimate and too creepy. *Maybe the helmet didn't totally protect my head because I'm clearly losing it.*

My bladder protests, and I realize that I desperately have to pee. I'm about to move when I'm suddenly struck with the thought that I don't know how I got back after my last bathroom trip. I remember my standoff with Alpha, but it all goes fuzzy afterward.

Shaking my head, I decide not to worry about it for now.

I don't want to disturb Danny, so I scoot over to the left side of the bed and start to work the blanket off of my legs. My body trembles from a mixture of pain and lack of movement as I lift myself into an upright position. The room tilts and does a little spin, forcing me to swallow back the bile splashing in the back of my throat.

Once the wave passes, I take a deep breath, use the nightstand for support, and push myself up. My arms quake, and a shot of pain fires through my casted leg. I try to clench my jaw, but the muffled scream of pain still echoes out in the room. *Dang it.*

"Beatrice? What are you doin', woman? You're not supposed to be moving on your own. Here, let me." Danny's words are rushed and playful. I expected aggression like Alpha, but Danny is still being sweet and annoyingly wonderful.

Shaking my head, I insist, "No, no. I've got it. You go back to reading your book. I'm fine." Unfortunately for me, the word fine comes out way too high as another shot of pain threatens to take me out. Sparks filter behind my eyes as the pain causes another wave of dizziness.

Before it fully passes, my whole world tilts, and I'm being lifted in the air. "Danny!" I screech. "Put me down! I can walk! I'm too heavy for you!" I sound ridiculous, high-pitched, and indignant, but not strong in my convictions at all.

"No can do, My Flower. I've got you. And, if you ever say some stupid shit like that again, healing or not, I'll pull you over my lap and give you a pretty, pink handprint on your ass to remind you that you're fucking perfect." How someone who is so playful and so carefree can turn dominant mid-sentence is a phenomenon I never knew existed.

Stu showed his dominant side that night at the bar, and it had me completely entranced. But Danny... he went from playful to possessive really dang quick.

Clearly, I've been stunned stupid because we're already near the bathroom; and now I wonder if my panties are wet because he turned me on or if I peed myself? Good Lord knows that's all I need right now.

Danny steps into the bathroom and carefully sets me down. When I have a good hold of the counter, he jumps up. "Ooo, I forgot! Be right back!" His smile is wide and infectious, and his eyes sparkle with excitement.

I assume he's going to leave, but he doesn't. Instead, he grabs my face, kisses the living crap out of me, then smiles wider and bounds down the hall. The whiplash has me wide-eyed and my mouth gaping. I'm pretty sure I look like a surprised owl right now. *What the fork just happened?*

I don't have time to dissect it because he comes barreling down the hall again with a little duffle bag slung over his shoulder. *Wait a second. That's mine!*

My surprise must be blatant across my face as he grins cheekily and sets the bag on the bathroom counter. "Figured you'd want your own stuff, so I grabbed some of your bathroom shit while Stu grabbed your clothes, and the other 2 packed up the things Stu told them to find."

He says it so dang casually, like it was a run to the grocery store, and not at all creepy that four men I don't trust- and currently hate- were going through my things.

So many emotions battle in my mind as I try to find one and hold onto it. Pain, loss, anger, sadness, betrayal... it's all too much. It's all too overwhelming.

An ugly sob bursts from my chest, and tears flood my face. Danny's blurry form moves closer to me, and he wraps me in his arms, quietly shushing me while rubbing my back.

We stand like that, me losing control and him fighting to help me regain it for what seems like an eternity. I felt my knees buckle a while ago, but he's held me up, held me together; and that makes me feel simultaneously better and worse.

I'm not this woman. I don't need others to help me. I've lived life so long, basically alone. *But why does it feel so darn good to be held?*

Eventually, my sobs turn into muffled hiccups. Danny slowly releases me but doesn't move back. His soft hands caress my face as he swipes away the remaining tears. His lips tip up in a gentle grin before he brings his forehead to rest on mine. "It's ok. You're going to be ok. I promise."

And for some reason, I believe him.

I gulp in a deep breath, count to four, then release it.

He lifts his head away from mine, and his nose crinkles adorably. "You're sexy as hell and beautiful no matter what... but you may want to brush your teeth." His face scrunches hilariously, and I can't stop the watery giggle that bursts out of me.

"Oh my God! I'm so sorry!" I cover my mouth and squeal with a mixture of embarrassment and giddiness.

He chuckles and steps around me. "While you do that, I'm going to run you a bath."

My whole body freezes. "A-a bath?"

"Of course. You can't get your casts wet, so I'll wrap them first, but I'm sure you'd like to get clean. It's been six days since your accident."

Holy schnitzel! Six days! That's gross and terrifying, and overwhelming, and-

"Easy, My Flower. It's ok. I've got a lavender bubble bath to cover you, and when you're ready, I'll wash your hair."

"Huh?!" I squeak out. "Wh-why would you do that?"

I turn to face the mirror, catching our reflections as he steps up next to me. "Because you need help. And I'd do anything for you. We all would."

I scoff and roll my eyes. "You're wrong about that. Alpha friggin' hates me. I didn't even do anything to him."

Then, the thought strikes me down like lightning hitting a tree. It's been six days, and I haven't seen Stu once. I mean, yes, I'm mad and hurt, but... we were friends once. Right? *Or was that a lie, too?*

Danny's far too perceptive for his own good. He rubs a hand over my shoulder and whispers, "He needs some time. He's..." His eyes seem to be searching deep inside for the right words. "He's hurting. He just needs some time."

I feel the scowl form on my face. *What the fork is he hurting for? I didn't betray him, I didn't lie to him, and I'm the one who got hurt. In more than ten ways!*

The rush of bath water brings me out of my head, and I look over to see Danny pouring in a heaping amount of something that smells absolutely divine.

I unzip the bag and pull out my toothbrush and toothpaste. The sensation of scrubbing away the grime and muck from my mouth is almost orgasmic.

Once I'm finished, Danny opens the toilet seat and brushes past me. "Holler at me when you're done, and I'll get you wrapped up."

Without a backward glance, he closes the door; leaving me alone with my thoughts and the heavenly aroma of the steaming bath.

It takes Danny and I about fifteen minutes to get situated. After going to the bathroom, Danny came back to wrap my casts. Then, we had a brief argument about him helping me into the tub; one I eventually lost as I slipped trying to hobble out of his grasp.

I made him bring me a towel to cover with, and, of course, he smirked and raked his gaze up and down my body.

Yeah, yeah. I know he's obviously seen me naked, but that was under false pretenses, and that's not happening again.

The bubbles would probably cover everything, but as I get in, I'm glad I have the towel. It felt a little like a piece of armor still protecting my heart from the men who run this house.

Eventually, he talked me into allowing him to carry me and slowly submerge my body in the water. At first, it freaking hurt. It *all* freaking hurt. I can't lie, though; I'm glad he helped. I definitely would have injured myself further had I been left on my own.

My right arm is now resting on the tub's ledge and my left leg is, basically, sticking straight up and over the tub; my toes peeking out of the plastic so they can get cleaned, too. Thankfully, the cast goes just a few inches past my knee, so I'm still able to have a full bath.

Danny disappeared a couple of minutes ago to "grab some stuff," which allowed me to finally sink in and relax in the awesomeness that is this bath. I know I've been riddled with nightmares, and sweating profusely, so the warm lavender water feels like a healing balm.

A gentle knock comes from the door, and Danny pokes his head in with a wide smile as if he just found his parents' secret candy stash. *Goofy dork is too cute for words.*

"Hello, Gorgeous." He toddles in, and I can't help but giggle.

"You act like you didn't just see me three minutes ago." I smile, shaking my head. His response is just a shy shrug as he looks away. I see his pale skin flush. *Oh my gosh! Is he, for real, blushing? Why is that attractive?*

Before I can comment, he clears his throat and holds up a big, purple loofah- with tags still on it- and what appears to be some kind of hose with a showerhead nozzle. I tilt my head and try really hard to get my brain to understand what he's doing with it. He must see my extreme confusion because he chuffs a laugh and says, "This is to help get you clean," he holds up the loofah and shakes it around. "I figured you'd rather that than my actual hand since it's going to be hard for you to maneuver with only one arm and one leg in use." I feel the blood drain from my face as I realize that he wants to clean me. Is there no way I can do it myself? I mean, how hard can it b-

His voice cuts off my swirling anxiety as he holds up the hose with the shower head. "And this is so I can clean your hair. Don't want you to move too much, so it won't be a good idea to dunk you. That, and I'm pretty sure you want to do that after we get the dirty bath water out of there."

He pauses for all of two seconds before his eyes widen. "Not that you're dirty, you're perfect, just that, you know..."

Darn it. He's too cute. I grin at how quickly he jumps from confident to silly to unsure. He's too freaking adorable. I kind of hate it. *No, you don't.*

"Danny," I say quietly, my smile stretching so wide it actually hurts. "It's fine." I take a deep breath and settle further into the tub before whispering, "Thank you. For everything."

I peer up at him through my lashes and see him shaking his head before he steps toward the tub. My whole body goes taut like a tight rope as he kneels next to the tub and rips the tag off the loofah with his teeth. *Oh, cheese-its. Now, something else tightened.*

Danny, completely unaware of my inner turmoil, dunks the loofah in the warm water, then pops back up to my bag. He rummages around before pulling out my Champagne Toast body wash from Bath and Body Works. After applying a generous dollop, he kneels next to me again, rubbing the loofah until it's nice and bubbly.

Neither of us speaks as he lifts my left foot and gently cleans the little bit of my foot sticking out of my cast. A giggle tinkles out of my mouth, and I slip further into the water. Danny's eyes widen in surprise as a full smile forms across his perfect face. "Is my Flower ticklish?" It's completely rhetorical because he swipes the loofah across my foot again, and I squeal out as I try not to kick in response. His answering laugh is dang near musical, and I wish I could hear it every day.

I flick water at him, causing him to flinch back in surprise. His eyes widen and he looks aghast as his mouth drops in shock.

"Be careful startin' shit with me, Flower. I'll be forced to finish." The gleam in his eyes tells me he's being playful, but I swear his voice dipped a little lower. My pussy clenches in response, and I feel my own eyes widen, hoping to God he has no idea what his words did to me.

His eyes dilate, and his nostrils flare, showing me he knows exactly what just happened. *Jerkface.*

Thankfully, I'm in the bath, so if I turn into a puddle of goo, I can just slide right down the drain.

He breaks eye contact first, shaking his head to clear whatever images he had playing out in his mind. I feel my face burn brighter and kind of wish I could sink underneath the bubbles.

Danny bends over the tub and glides the loofah over my foot and up my leg in small, circular motions. I tense as he hits the top of my thigh, right next to where the soaked towel is covering my mound. But he doesn't say anything. He doesn't *do* anything. Instead, he skips over it entirely and begins working on my arms. He cleanses my right arm first; well the parts that are *not* covered by plastic. His heady scent, a combination of leather and eucalyptus, swirls into my nose, and I have to actively hold back a groan.

Memories of *that* night streak through my mind.

Looking back on it, It's so obvious that it was them, and I feel like a total idiot for missing it.

His voice in my ear talking about taking Even's pierced cock in his ass. The feeling of his lips nipping and sucking along my neck and jaw while Even worked my pussy, Alpha tortured my clit, and Stu...*friggin' Stu kissed me!*

Danny continues his ministrations, rubbing the loofah all over my arms, shoulder, chest... I close my eyes and let myself just remember. Remember the last time I was so dang happy; before it all went to crap on a cracker.

Danny and Stu had their hands on my breasts while I squeezed their hard, pierced cocks. I bite my lip, thinking about how they would feel in my mouth, how they would taste.

Something fluffy, yet kinda rough, brushes over my nipple in my mind. I can't place it in my memory, but I gasp out in surprise. The feeling causes my pussy to clench, and I almost moan out. Thankfully, Danny doesn't say anything, so I'm hoping he just thinks I'm completely relaxed and content and not at all acting like a horny slut.

Returning to my memory, I think about my arms being tied down and how free I felt to let go. To feel so safe and secure that I could just let everything else fall away.

Danny's hand slides down my body, over the towel, and my eyes open to find him staring into my dang soul. Our breaths are coming out in sharp pants, and I flush from the embarrassment of being caught.

"I-I'm, uh. I'm sorry. Just tired or som-" Danny cuts me off with his lips pressed against mine. The move is sudden and so unexpected that I can't do anything but stare in shock. His tongue traces the seam of my lips once, twice, before he breaks the connection. He doesn't go far though, and our breaths mingle as we toe the line of indecency. "Let me help you, Flower. Let me help you relax." I feel his fingers ghosting over the towel down my stomach and resting just at the top of my mound.

A war rages inside of me. But then I remember how good he feels. And, dang it, it's just sex. It's not like any of them are mine, so what's the harm in a little fun?

Especially since I'm trapped here indefinitely.

He must see my impending answer because he slams his lips against mine. The brutal passion lights a fire deep inside me, and I close my eyes, allowing myself this moment of reprieve. I can't regret it later, but for now...

His fingers find my mound through the sopping wet towel weighing on my body. His fingers firmly explore my hood, my lips, my everything...except my dang clit.

I growl in frustration and try to thrust my hips up to meet his fingers, but I can't do much in the sunken starfish position. His throaty chuckle vibrates my body, and I swear I feel myself get wet.

Just, you know, not from the bath.

His tongue plunders my mouth and tangles with mine. His minty flavor makes my mouth water, and I suck his tongue wholly into my mouth, moving up and down like I want to do with his cock. He groans low and deep, and I grin around his tongue, knowing I'm affecting him at least half as much as he's affecting me.

I'm so turned on I swear to God I would climb this man like a tree if he let me.

His fingers dance their way to the hem of the towel. With a flick of his wrist, the towel flips up and flops over on my stomach. His fingers find their way under my hood and expertly spread my lips wide. I tremble with anticipation as his pointer and ring fingers hold me wide open for him, and he uses his middle finger to swipe me from opening to clit.

I jerk with the attention and moan into his mouth.

His tongue snakes out and traces my lips before nipping on my lower one and sucking it into his mouth. The second his teeth make contact, he plunges two fingers deep into my pussy, and I moan embarrassingly loud.

My breaths are coming out as harsh pants as he begins pumping in and out of me. The heel of his palm connects with my clit as his fingers screw into me harder and harder. The pressure causes me to see spots behind my eyelids.

I feel his warm breath skate across my neck as Danny whispers, "That's it, Precious Flower, milk my fingers like you would my cock."

Even though the bath is warm, I feel goosebumps break out across my skin like tiny pinpricks.

He kisses my neck before sucking a section into his mouth. A third finger is added at the same time he releases my neck with a *pop*, then smooths away the sting with his tongue.

And. I. Lose it.

My brain turns to mush as a tsunami roars through my body and crashes through my pussy. My neck arches across the tub behind me, and I accidentally slam my casted arm into the wall.

But the pain doesn't register; not the way it should. Instead, it heightens the pleasure, and another orgasm rolls through me.

Danny's lips find mine in the sweetest kiss that's both languid and passionate; unhurried yet desperate. His kiss helps bring me down as his fingers continue to lazily pump in and out of my core, ringing out every aftershock possible before he gently removes them.

With a final kiss, he rises to stand, his cock straining against his jeans, and steps back.

For the next couple of minutes, he fiddles with connecting the hose to the shower nozzle, then pulls the drain plug.

He takes his time shampooing and conditioning my hair with the reverence of a friend, of a lover, and it brings tears to my eyes.

Once he's rinsed it all out, he lifts up, turns off the water, and grabs a towel. Placing the dry towel down before whipping off the wet one underneath, he carefully ensures that I'm all covered up before bending down and scooping me up; as if it's not awkward to pick someone up from a tub.

My arms hook around his neck, and I absent-mindedly twirl the lower curls of his hair at the base of his neck. My eyes close as I lean my head on his shoulder, inhaling his scent as I continue playing with his hair.

After helping me dry off, completely respectfully, he helped me into another pair of PSD boxers, chortling at the 90s cartoon characters. Then, he slipped an oversized nightdress over my head, handed me a hairbrush, and bounced out of the room in search of water, meds, and some lunch.

I had just enough time to eat lunch and watch a little bit of Grey's Anatomy with Danny before passing out.

And in the darkness, all the good feelings and happy endorphins disappeared.

~CHAPTER 11~

I'm more irritated than I usually would be while I make my way down to the dungeon. Apparently, Charlie and Stu grabbed a new target for HQ. They did all the recon, information digging, and capturing within 48 hours. I'm sure HQ is happy. But I was less than pleased when Even came in and ordered me to go down to my fun room while he looks after Beatrice.

Slamming the door open, I scan my hand and impatiently wait for the hidden door to unlock. The second it's open, I bound down the cement steps before coming to stand in front of my new toy. Charlie's leaning against the left wall, arms crossed over his chest like he's a bodyguard looking out for a high-profile celebrity or some shit.

Once Charlie notices me, he pushes off the wall and stalks toward us. "Danny, I'd like to introduce you to your new punching bad. *Bryce Benson.* Bryce here loves to call himself a Dom and *teaches* new subs how to behave properly." The malevolence in his tone surprises me a little. I can read between the lines as well as the next person, and, yeah, this guy is absolutely about to get what he deserves. But I've never heard Charlie sound anything except perfectly succinct with as little emotion as possible.

Either this guy and his bullshit really got to him, or Beatrice is way more under his skin than he's trying to let on.

With a nod, I tower over the sniveling bastard shackled to my steel table. Ripping off the duct tape, I feel my beast take over. "Hello Brycey-Poo. How has your stay been so far? Are the accommodations up to your expectations?"

He's blubbering the whole time, so I'm fairly certain that he didn't hear a single word I said.

No matter, he'll start talking soon enough.

I turn to my surgical tray, lined with all my favorite tools, and pick up a scalpel. "How many?" I shout to Charlie.

After a moment of silence, I glare up at Charlie. "Seventeen known."

I feel a grin crawl across my face as I look deep into Fuckboy's shit-brown eyes. "Wow! 17! Were there others?"

I lean over, letting the light glint off the scalpel right near his eyes. Tears pour down his chiseled cheeks, and his eyes widen as they track my progress.

"How many!" I yell in his face, causing him to jump.

When he still doesn't answer, I push my finger over his top, right eyelid, closing it shut, then slice it clean off. His screams ricochet off the walls around us, and it fills me with so much joy that my dick gets almost as hard as it does when I'm around my Precious Flower.

I vaguely hear Charlie grunt, followed by the sounds of his heavy ass steps leading up the stairs. Which reminds me...

"Hey, Boss Man..." I call out, glancing over my shoulder.

He stops between the fourth and fifth steps and faces me. His face is a mask of indifference, but I push on. "She calls out for you. You and Stu. Well, she calls you Alpha, but you know what

I mean. Her nightmares, boss..." I trail off, shaking my head as I think about the last few days of holding her in my arms as she screamed through the nightmares plaguing her.

"They're bad. And *she calls* for you. For both of you. I know the letter...fuck...I know it was fucked up, but she needs you. Whether you want her to or not. She needs you. Don't let Cammy ruin something that has the potential to be absolutely life-altering."

With a sigh, I turn around, let my beast take back over, and focus on Bryce *fucking* Benson.

~CHAPTER 12~

Charlie

This was one of our faster turnarounds, and I should be happy. Thrilled even. Easy cases keep our team at the top of the company pyramid; they also keep us the highest paid.

But, today, I'm not happy. Not even close. Danny telling me that I needed to visit Bea pissed me off. Beatrice living in our house pisses me off. Hell, the amount of times I have to consciously remove her from my mind pisses me off.

I'm not going to see her. As far as I'm concerned, she's Danny and Even's problem.

She annihilated Stu's heart. He hasn't been the same since he got the fucking letter. Well, really, he hasn't been the same since she kicked us out of her house all those weeks ago. She's a selfish, self-righteous, conniving little vix-, "Hhheellpp! Alpha! P-please, Alpha!"

I bust through the basement door, immediately on edge as adrenaline floods my body. I don't think; just react. Sprinting through the kitchen and living room, I race towards her room.

As I cross the threshold, I scan the area for intruders. , but I come up short when I see she's alone. *All. Fucking. Alone.* And thrashing violently in the bed. Her back arches as she screams out in agony. *Fuck, she's going to break something else.*

She's fighting off some invisible attacker, and I'm completely frozen. *What the hell do I do? Am I supposed to do something?*

"Allpphhaaaa!" The pure, unadulterated pain laced in her raspy voice pushes me to move. My mind plays back to what Stu did a few weeks ago when she had a night terror. I don't bother second-guessing; she's going to hurt herself if she doesn't calm down. I know I'm not supposed to wake her, but maybe I can at least help her settle.

Sliding into the bed, carefully avoiding her right hook, I squeeze her into me. A hiss of pain escapes through my teeth as her cast connects with my balls. But I push the pain away; pulling her closer into me, wrapping my arm across her chest, and tucking my hand around above her cast around her bicep.

Her body continues to convulse as she screams out in terror. I don't know how to comfort anyone. Not anymore. So, I just squeeze my eyes closed and start humming whatever song pops into my mind.

Something warm and wet begins to slide down my cheeks, and I quickly realize that I'm crying. The song I'm humming, the song that kills me the most, is All I Want by Kodaline. I consider forcing myself to stop, but I feel Beatrice slowly calming. Her body slowly releases the tension it's been holding onto, her breaths even out, and her rapid eye movement slows.

I shudder in a deep breath, close my eyes again, and begin to sing the words. I allow myself a moment to release the pain from losing Cammy; and the pain from knowing we, *I mean they,* almost lost Beatrice.

Eventually, she shifts her head and nuzzles sweetly against my forehead as her soft, adorable little snores take the place of her screaming in panic. Her forehead is warm and clammy against mine, and I find myself pulling her even closer against me as I continue to sing.

I'm just going to have this one moment. This moment to relax a little. This moment to not be angry at the world. Just this one moment to hold her in my arms the way I desperately wanted to before all of this happened. *Pfft. Before. Right...*

~CHAPTER 13~

Sitting outside of Bea's room, waiting for Danny to finish in the basement, I find myself oddly filled with *jealousy*.

I had to go to the bathroom earlier while Danny and Charlie were downstairs. Stu has been noticeably MIA since the day we found the letter.

But, while I was in there, I heard her terrified screams. And, damn, hearing her screaming out, knowing I was supposed to be there, gutted me. *Of course* my body decided that was the moment I needed to relieve myself, so she was left vulnerable, scared, and all alone.

Her screaming for "Alpha" though... I'm starting to think their little "video sessions" meant a whole lot more to both of them than they let on.

By the time I finished and got cleaned up, I turned the corner to find Charlie snuggled against a calm, serene-looking Beatrice. His arm was draped across her body, and the fingers poking out of her cast were hooked onto his forearm. Her head was leaning against his, and they both looked oddly at peace. But the craziest damn part was seeing Charlie had fucking fallen asleep!

He can't sleep with anyone touching him. Hell, he can't sleep 90% of the time alone in his room. Between his childhood, his time serving as a Marine, and what happened with Cammy, he's a certified Insomniac. How much he can get done on so little sleep is freaky.

Not wanting to disturb them, I swiped my tablet from the nightstand and meandered back to the hallway where Danny had moved the armchair. With a loud sigh, I slid in and started working on my latest compilation of words; poems, I guess.

Thirty minutes later, I'm still sitting here while Charlie snuggles Beatrice. And, yes, I have realized I am a little jealous. I should have been there. *Me*. Charlie couldn't comfort an abandoned puppy, let alone a human being. That ability switched off a long ass time ago. But here we are. He's ignored her for days, belittled her, made it very clear he doesn't want her here... And yet, he's in there, right now, cuddled up with her.

It's both adorable and infuriating.

A door slams down the hall, and I assume it's Danny because Stu rarely leaves his room anymore. The quiet footsteps are rushed, almost frantic, and I stand, ready for a fight.

I hate this part.

Danny flies around the corner, his eyes darker than his hair, as he frantically searches around me. "Where?" He growls low and menacing.

A little tingle shivers down my spine. It's always hard to get his beast back in its cage, but now I have to worry about him accidentally hurting Bea.

Danny's the most gentle, loving soul, but his beast...yeah, not so much. When he's trapped in the red place, we've found one *specific* thing that helps bring him back quickly.

But I'm not sure if I can distract him long enough to lead him away from Bea.

Placing both hands up, I quickly slide in front of the doorway and gently close the door. Placing both of my hands up in a placating gesture, I firmly state, "She's sleeping." I almost tell him she had a nightmare but decide he may lose it if he knows she was sad or scared without him here. *Dude, same.*

What I don't anticipate is the growl he releases and his lip tipping up into a sneer as he comes toe-to-toe with me. "Move."

My brows raise all the way to my hairline at his insistence. Flicking my gaze between his eyes, I see that he's completely in the red place and is not going to give up easily.

But I can't let him wake Bea. I won't. *Shit, this is going to be much harder than I thought.*

Letting my hands barely touching his chest, I try again. My voice is calm, firm, but I do raise it just a little, hoping I can wade through the haze he's in. "No. Beatrice needs to sleep so she can get better. *You,*" I point near his face, keeping my right hand resting on his chest, "need to get cleaned up and eat something before seeing her."

And this motherfucker swings.

A loud crack resounds through the hall, and I belatedly realize that it's my jaw.

By the next swing, I'm ready. My right hand darts out in time to catch the outside of his right wrist; locking on tight. With my other hand, I push his right arm just below his shoulder, then abruptly pull his arm across his body. Before he can react, I'm shoving his chest against the wall, wrenching his arms behind him, and interlocking his wrists in my hand.

Danny roars out in blind rage and thrashes wildly against the wall and me. "Silent, Baby Boy." I hiss in his ear. "Stop, Now!"

His body trembles. Then, I feel every muscle in his body slowly unlocks. Knowing his mind is almost ready to proceed, I take his earlobe in my mouth and bite down, eliciting a harsh gasp and a partial growl from him.

"No!" I snap, popping him on the ass with my full hand. A throaty moan falls from his mouth, and his head thumps against the wall with a dull *thud*.

"I know you want to see Beatrice, but right now, *you're* not in control. I am," I growl as I thrust my jean-clad erection against the top of his ass.

"Y-yes, sir." His words come out as a croak, sounding painfully raspy.

"Good, boy." I grit through my teeth. I take a half step back and maneuver his hands until they are right against my belt. "Now, take off my belt, and free my fucking cock."

His body vibrates with need as he quickly fiddles with the buckle, unclasping it just a heartbeat before he flicks the button on my jeans and unzips my zipper. His warm, soft hands make their way under my briefs, and I can't help the groan that rumbles out of me.

"Are you going to be a good boy?" I rasp as he rubs his fingers across the tip of my dick; flicking the Prince Albert back and forth a few times before giving the top half of my dick a hard tug.

"Good. So good. I p-promise." His hips thrust violently against the wall in front of him. The involuntary thrusting shows me that my sweet Danny Boy's beast is almost locked up tight.

With a smirk, I lick a path from the pulse point on his neck all the way to his ear, flicking it lightly before biting down.

His whole body quakes against mine, and I briefly lose my ability to focus on anything but my need to feel his tight ass choking my cock.

"Hands on the wall," I command. He obeys immediately, earning a low groan of approval. Reaching my arms around his waist, I quickly strip his pants from his body, silently thanking God, again, that this crazy man hates wearing underwear.

My hands shake as I squeeze my cock, lazily pumping with one hand as my other spreads his cheeks apart. "Wall pose." My bark causes him to jump, but he quickly obeys.

With a grace that a man shouldn't possess, his hands slide down the wall as he lowers his upper body and sticks his sexy ass out for me to ogle. I give him an appreciative hum, sucking my bottom lip into my mouth and biting down.

I lean over, spread his sexy ass cheeks wide, and spit right at his hole. "I don't have lube, but you have a safeword. What is it?"

I continue massaging the globes of his ass, and his legs shiver with anticipation before he grunts, "Smorgasbord."

Satisfied, I part his cheeks before spitting in my hand. Rubbing it along my shaft, I nudge the tip at his entrance then whisper, "Come back to me, Baby Boy. I've got you."

Pushing past the tight ring, I pop in the head of my throbbing cock.

Our groans echo down the hall as I slowly slide all the way into his tight channel. "Yes, Love. Fuck me. Please." Danny's whispered words are mixed with pain and pleasure; soothing my soul in the best way.

With the confirmation that he's back with me, that his beast is locked firmly away, I begin to plow into him.

Sweat drips from my brow and lands on his ass, and I swear I hear it sizzle. *Ok, maybe not, but his ass is so damn hot.*

Within mere moments, my balls are drawing up, and I feel the base of my spine tingle. Keeping one hand on his hip, I use the other to curl my arm in front of Danny and stroke him in time with my thrusts. "Good boy. You did so well not cumming with my fat cock deep in your ass. You ready to come with me, Baby Boy?"

His mewled response sets me off, and I feel jet after jet of my sticky cum plaster deep inside his cavity.

As I come down from the high of the orgasm, I feel the same warm-sticky substance dripping from my hand. Thankfully, it feels like I caught most of Danny's release in my hand, so I won't have to deal with Charlie bitchin' about the mess.

With a pat on his ass, I slowly remove my soaking cocking from Danny and step back. Keeping my fist closed to prevent any more from spilling, I wait for him to turn around so I can kiss the shit out of him.

But I don't get that chance. When Danny turns, his cock slowly deflating, and looking absolutely, deliciously fucked, his eyes widen, he sucks in a deep breath, and freezes completely.

"Uh...I... just... the bathroom..." I hear Bea's sweet fucking voice moments before I hear her casted leg thumping quickly down the hall. She closes the door gently before we hear a *thud* against the door.

Danny's eyes are as wide as saucers as they slowly move to meet my equally shocked gaze.

And, then, the asshole laughs.

I don't mean a chuckle, a chortle, a snicker. No, this mother fucker full-on, gasping for breath, maniacally loud, hysterically laughs. I'm still too stunned to react because *what the fuck just happened?*

As his laughter subsides, I'm still standing there, limp noodle out, fist full of cum. Suddenly, he hauls me by my collar and thrusts his tongue into my mouth. It doesn't take long before I'm giving as good as I get; our tongues dueling for dominance.

Just when I think I may pass out from lack of air, he breaks the kiss; his smile wide and a little goofy. "She *totally* liked that.

You didn't see her face. She was definitely standing there for a bit." He whispers, and a conspiratorial gleam crosses his gaze.

Shaking my head, I smile back and hope he's at least somewhat right. I mean, she was turned on by Danny talking about me fucking him. But hearing about it and seeing it are two different things. *Fuck.*

~CHAPTER 14~

*H*oly cock and balls that was so hot. *Like melting popsicles during a Texas heatwave, or giant bonfires on a crisp, Fall night.*

It takes me a ridiculous amount of time to cool off after seeing Even fuck Danny into submission. I'm not sure what was hotter: Even's ridiculously dirty words, or Danny presenting in wall pose.

I waited an obnoxiously long time to leave the bathroom after relieving my bladder. Thankfully, when I peered out into the hall, the two sexy men had disappeared.

Of course, my soaked panty problem didn't go away as quickly as I hoped because Alpha was still sleeping softly in my bed when I returned. I spent way too long debating on whether I should climb back into bed with him or not.

When I first woke up with a very full bladder, I was completely caught off guard by the very large, warm, monster sleeping next to me. I had no idea when he came in, or why, but my bladder was surely going to burst. I quickly decided to slip out instead of accidentally waking the man-beast.

Coming back from the bathroom was a very different story. I hovered at the end of the bed for the longest time before taking up residence on the chaise. It took me a hell of a long time to get comfortable, and I really missed my big blanket, but I didn't want to startle the man who currently hates me.

Although, I still can't figure out why.

From my spot in front of the window, I can see the gorgeous pool rippling from the soft breeze as the clouds move briskly across the sky. By the looks of it, we've had our first cool front of our yearly "Fake Fall". Yes, it's weird. But ask anyone who lives near Houston: we get a brief glimpse of Fall temps every year before another summer-like heat snap.

I wish I felt comfortable going outside, but I'm still unsteady on this bulky forking cast and I refuse to ask for help to take a walk. These men are doing enough as it is. Too much if you ask me.

Alpha murmurs in his sleep, pulling my attention from the oasis that is their backyard. He doesn't look as mean and grumpy in his sleep. The scowl he seems to wear regularly is gone, the little crinkle between his brows that's usually present has magically disappeared, and he looks so... *normal.*

Watching a relaxed Alpha is way better than the jerkface Alpha I'm, sort of, coming to know. I miss the old Alpha. The one who made me feel not-so-weird, not-so-ugly, and not-so-useless.

I've been chatting with a man through a "sexy video" site I found. Sometimes, I don't have time to vet and meet men in person and I absolutely cannot get myself off when I'm alone.

It also helps that I can still hide my face while I get off on looking at tasty man candy.

Tonight, the man, whose profile name is Cap, and I decided to finally meet through webcam.

Suddenly, a sound echoes from the computer just before he comes into view. Well, the spot between his neck and belly button does. And, holy delicious gumballs, what a view it is.

"H-Hi," I squeak like a little schoolgirl.

His throaty chuckle rings out and I swear the sound waves vibrate deep into my core. Squeezing my thighs together, I am suddenly thankful that I'm wearing my deep purple mask that covers most of my cheeks because, right now, they're bright friggin' red.

"Nice to finally meet you." His voice is sweet and thick like syrup and I suddenly have a desire for pancakes. Or... licking pancakes off his ridiculously built mid-section.

"Uh, you too. I mean, it's nice to meet you, too." I stumble over my words like an idiot.

He clears his throat, bringing me out of my self-conscious state. "So, I was thinking. Um, you're profile said you like reading fiction and fantasies. Any chance you dapple with Omegaverse?"

His question catches me totally off guard because, actually, yes I do, but part of it is because reverse harem romances are plentiful in Omegaverse books. Contemporary reverse harem romances really became a thing in the last decade, so there aren't a whole lot to choose from. That, and, I totally relate to an Omega's need to nest. Hence my ridiculous obsession with soft, fuzzy blankets... and all three of my weighted blankets. Heck, I even leave the house cooler than it needs to be so I can curl up in a blanket.

After far too long, I admit that I like Omegaverses.

Of course, Mr. Tall, Swole, and Growly identified most with alphas. Sadly, I haven't had the greatest track record with people that refer to themselves as "alphas". But this is through video, and he can't hurt me, so he can be whatever, or whomever, he wants to be.

That was the day we permanently changed our names to Alpha and Omega. That was also the day I orgasmed with my legs spread wide for a man looking through a webcam, with nothing more than my fingers. It was intense, insane, and completely mind-bending.

We met at least twice a month, every month after that. We didn't set dates in advance, and I never reached out; I never wanted to seem needy.

But I swear he had an uncanny ability to know when I needed him most.

Now that I'm staring at this cruel, beautiful giant, I don't see the Alpha I became *fond* of. I see a man who thinks he's an alpha but is really just a big bully.

And, here I am, trapped in a house with him. *Awesome*.

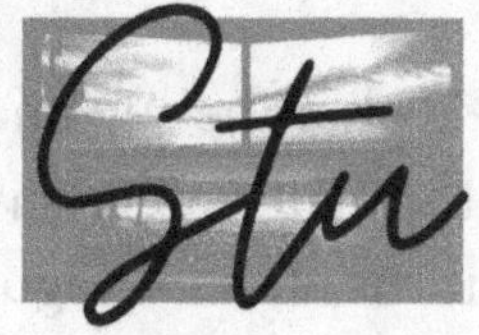

Beatrice has been here for over a week and I still haven't gone down to see her. Not since I read her letter. *That damn letter.*

Tears spring to my eyes as her words come back to haunt me. She loved me. But, she was going to leave me.

A notification pings on my computer, dragging me out of another vortex of pain. My stomach grumbles as I move the mouse around, barely comprehending the words on the screen. It looks like we have a new lead for the Crimson Knights. *Awesome. I guess.*

God, even my thoughts are morose.

Flinging my chair back, I walk out the door in search of Charlie. Before I know it, I'm smacking head-first into a guilty-looking Even. Danny's trailing behind him with a smug look of satisfaction spread across his face.

"Uh, hey, just going to clean up." I tilt my head, and my brow, trying to figure out why he has to clean up. Danny's our torture tech, and Even was on Beatrice duty. *Wait...*

"Who's with Bea?" I inquire, a hint of panic evident in my voice.

Danny steps forward, slapping his hand against my shoulder. "Lighten up, Stu boy. Charlie's with her."

I explode with fury at the thought of the one person in this house, who hates her very presence, being alone in a room with her.

"Are you insane? He'll chew her up and spit her out!"

I'm running down the hall before giving either of them a chance to speak. As I hit the stairs, I vaguely hear Even yell out, "He's sleeping!"

That makes no sense. Charlie seldom sleeps. Besides, *if he's with her, where is he sleeping? How?*

My feet seem to hover over the floor as I jump down the last few stairs and sprint to the back of the house. Once I reach the guest room, I suddenly come to a halt at the threshold as I take in the room. I'm so damn confused that it takes me way too long to piece together what I'm seeing.

Charlie is passed smooth out on the bed Bea was sleeping in. Her navy blue weighted blanket is pressed around him as he sleeps, absolutely oblivious to the world around him.

Shit. I don't think I've ever seen him look so...so...*relaxed.*

Movement near the window catches my eye and I see Bea partially curled up on the chaise, watching the trees sway in the distance. The little bit of light coming in from the cloudy, November sky casts her in an almost ethereal glow.

My heart squeezes painfully, and a half whimper seeps from my chest.

Her head whips around, eyes wide like an all-seeing owl, and I notice her chest skip a few times. My gaze is riveted to hers and I suddenly forget how to think, how to breathe, how to function. *Shit.*

"You're here." There's a hint of accusation in her voice; as if she's noticed my purposeful absence.

Unable to take the guilt, I look over her shoulder and out the window, as a beam of sunlight strikes through the clouds.

Clearing my throat, I weakly deflect, "Was looking for Charlie. But he doesn't sleep much so I'll leave him be for now."

I turn to leave, but her raspy voice inquires, "Charlie?" The questioning tone stops me in my tracks. Looking back with what I'm sure is a puzzled face, she bows her head, a light pink tinging her soft cheeks, as she picks at the hem of her nightdress. "He, um, he never told me his name. He, he was Alpha and..." She sucks in a stuttered breath before continuing. "Um, he called me Omega. It's just," she shrugs a shoulder bashfully.

"Nice to know his actual name?" I finish for her. Her eyes snap to mine and widen again; almost like she forgot she was talking to me.

With a subtle nod, she glances away. The little sunbeam out the window catches her eyes in just the right way and I can see a small layer of tears gathering in her eyes.

Part of me wants to rush to comfort her, and another part of me wants to turn and run so I don't fall in love with her again. *Yeah, like you ever stopped.*

Everything is such a hot mess and I have no idea what to do, how to do it, or if she even wants me to do it. We went from being best friends to her being so pissed at me that she refused to talk to me, to a wild, passionate, insanely sexy night with my guys, to her almost dying.

Then...oh, and then...the goodbye letter.

"Stu," she whispers, bringing my attention back to her. "Why, um..." She bites that ridiculously plump lower lip as she gathers her thoughts.

After at least a minute, she still hasn't finished her thought. But, I know where she was going.

"Why haven't I spent time with you since you've been here?"

She sighs heavily, resuming her attention to the little thread hanging from her nightdress. With a subtle nod, she continues to keep her gaze down.

Swallowing the lump of wool that seems to have clogged my throat, I respond. "I, uh, didn't think you wanted to see me. We all decided to help you heal, but you were so mad, and then the night at the club... the way you looked at me..."

I angrily bat away a stray tear before shoving my hands into my hair and pulling, allowing the pain to ground me.

"Then, the letter. Bea, the letter hurt more than anything I've ever experienced. More than you hating me, more than you not forgiving me, more than...than...anything I've ever experienced." I peer at her from the corner of my eyes and see that she is completely perplexed.

Before I can go on, she tilts her head like I've lost my mind. "Letter? What are you talking about?"

Tears now stream freely down my cheeks. With the accident and everything else, she must have forgotten her plans. Or, at least, she doesn't remember having sent the letter in preparation.

The sudden intake of air sounds like a shotgun blast as she gasps in realization. "The letter!" She exclaims, throwing her un-casted arm over her eyes and falling against the chaise.

"The dang letter. Oh God. Oh G-God." Her breaths become labored and she slides to a sitting position with her feet on the ground. My breath quickens as she battles a panic attack.

Impulsively, I move forward, sliding onto the chaise next to her, wrapping an arm around her shoulders, and tugging her into me. Wrapping my other arm around her chest, I interlock my fingers and begin to sway us back and forth as sobs wrack her beautiful body. "Shhh, it's ok, Bea. It's ok. I've got you."

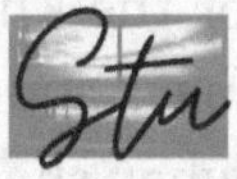

Twenty minutes later, we're lying on the chaise lounge together. She's curled up on my chest, casted arm resting across my mid-section, and her deep, steady breaths have lulled me into a sense of peace I wasn't sure I'd get again.

She may not have forgiven me for what happened that night at the club, yet, but she did let me arrange us more comfortably before she fell asleep in my arms.

Right where she's supposed to be.

Charlie begins to stir, mumbling incoherently. I keep my eyes closed, inhaling the scent that is all Bea, and soaking up however long she allows me to touch her.

Eventually, I crack an eye open when I hear him grunt, cursing under his breath. Peering over Bea's head, I see Charlie struggling to untangle himself from the weight of her blanket before oafishly landing on the ground with a loud "Oomph".

I try to suppress my laugh, but it comes out anyway. Although, it ends up being more of a chortle instead of a laugh. His eyes glare at me from the floor, then land on Bea's sleeping form. His glare recedes slightly before he runs his eyes over her body as if he's checking for more scratches or something.

With a grunt, he pulls himself up, petulantly kicking the blanket away, before standing to his full height. Locking eyes with mine, I see the questions, the concern, swirling through his. With, what I hope is, an assuring smile, I dip my chin toward Bea.

He seems reluctant as he nods in return, but doesn't press. "Oh, I have a new target for the Knights. Um," I look down at Bea, softly snoring into my neck and bit my cheek.

"It's fine. Come find me when she wakes up. Doc is coming by later to check on her and give her a PT plan."

My eyes widen, knowing how much she is going to hate that. But Charlie just chuckles before slinking out into the hallway.

Releasing a deep breath through my nose, I close my eyes and allow myself to have this moment with her.

God only knows how long it's going to last.

CHAPTER 16

I'm snuggled in a cocoon of warmth and light. I feel utterly exhausted, still, but, somehow, at peace. Although, I can't recall why. I haven't felt this calm since...

My eyes spring open to find a pair of bright blue eyes staring back at me. His forehead is resting against mine and I gulp loudly at the proximity. Even though I'm staring into his beautiful eyes, I can tell he's smiling. His cheeks are pushed up and they're causing his eyes to crinkle at the corners.

"Hi," I whisper in awe.

His cheeks rise more and his eyes sparkle with pure joy. *Dang I missed him.*

"Hi," he responds; a faint blush tinting his smooth cheeks. Shakily, I reach up my casted arm and rub a single finger over his left dimple. Looking back into his eyes, I see that his eyes were not on mine, but rather on my mouth. Unconsciously, I lick my lips, regretting how many meals and drinks I've stubbornly picked through.

Swallowing heavily, I lean forward. I need to feel his lips on mine. I need him to kiss me like I need my next breath. I need him to know I'm scared to be vulnerable. I need...

A knock on the door startles me and I dang near fall to the floor. Thankfully, Stu's like a cat. A big, pretty, goofy cat and he grabs my underarms just in time to slow my descent, allowing the padding of my behind to escape a brutal hit.

Stu quickly stands, his messy, dulled pink hair flopping over his eyes, and gently helps me to my feet. "You ok?" He probes. But, for some reason, his tone makes me think he's not just asking about my fall.

A voice clears behind me, and I yelp having forgotten someone had been standing there. I shift, facing the doorway, to find Doc standing there with a tight grin and a little bit of intrigue sparkling in his eyes.

"Doc! Good to see you." I smile, genuinely happy to see him. The faster I heal, the faster I can get out of *their* house.

I hear Stu shift next to me before he places a chaste kiss to the side of my head, momentarily stunning me.

I must blink ten times by the time he brushes past me, shakes hands with Doc, and exits the room.

Doc clears his throat and smiles pointedly. I feel myself blush and try to look away to escape his all-knowing gaze. "Um," I mumble. "What can I do you for?" I tried sounding nonchalant, but definitely sounded more like a bartender in the country.

He chuckles good-naturedly, then puts me out of my misery. Stepping forward, he waves at me to take a seat and explains that he just wants to check my healing progress and outline a physical therapy plan; ensuring my muscles don't atrophy.

An hour later, he leaves me with a warm hug, after asking if I wanted one, and encourages me to take it easy on the guys. He also states, again, that they're "good guys, with good intentions". *Whatever.* They're basically holding me hostage, so they can take their intentions and shove them up their rears.

The good news is, I'm healing pretty well. My cuts and scratches are mostly gone, and the bruising has faded tremendously; leaving a few ugly yellowish-green marks splattered across my body.

He also had a few things to say about my bull-headedness and basically sulking in my room. I chuffed and rolled my eyes, knowing full well that *Charlie* probably used those words, but I get it. I can't get better if I keep hiding in the room.

Deciding to change my attitude, for now, I open the bags in the corner and begin rummaging around for some clean clothes. I was a little, ok a lot, perturbed that someone, or multiple someones, went through my drawers and bathroom stuff, but at least I have my own things to change into.

Awkwardly flinging my bathroom bag over my shoulder, I scoop up my clothes, and hobble towards the bathroom. Arranging my shower crap along the shelves, I take out my shaving cream and razor. Obviously, I can't shave everything but I hate the feel of hair on my skin so, I can at least take care of some of it.

Eight minutes later, I'm shaved smooth and already feeling ridiculously better, but now I find myself completely befuddled.

It was semi-easy to sit, albeit strangely, on the edge of the tub to shave, but how do I clean my hair and body now? I'm not exactly the most limber woman, but having opposing casts on my body definitely makes things dang near impossible.

Grabbing a folded towel from under the vanity, I lie it on the floor next to the tub and turn the faucet back on; letting it re-warm while I consider how I'm going to do this successfully.

Leaning over, I line the tub with my shampoo, conditioner, and body wash then slip down onto the towel. Thankfully, I think, the faucet is on the right side of the tub, away from the toilet. Kneeling on my right leg, and being forced to extend my casted leg out toward the cabinet, I grunt as I bend over the ledge and dip my head under the running water.

The warmth cascades over me and I groan in appreciation. I deftly keep my right arm on the outside of the tub, preventing the water from hitting it. I reach toward the ledge to my left, blindly looking for the closest bottle before pumping the globby mixture into my hand and rubbing it through my hair. It's not perfect, but dang does it feel so friggin' good.

I even add in a good scraping of my nails and a half massage right before I rinse it out.

Gently lifting my head out of the water, I feel a rush of dizziness and groan out, clasping onto the side of the tub to catch myself. *Must have sat upright too fast.*

With a few deep, rejuvenating breaths, I pump a few globs of conditioner into my hand and work it through my hair, spending a little extra time massaging it in.

Once I'm satisfied that my hair is fully moisturized, I lean my hand under the water again.

Only, this time, the dizziness hits me right between the eyes and I lose my balance. Slamming down into the tub, I crack my head and hear myself shriek from the pain. But, now, my problem is that my leg cast is stuck on the ledge of the tub and the water is pouring over me like some kind of jacked-up water torture.

I try to scream but can't get anything other than garbled sounds. *Holy crackerjacks! I'm going to die.*

For some reason, I fight. I fight against the water, I fight to get my cast to raise above the tub, I fight to stop slipping every time I set my free arm down...

I just fight.

Through my panic, I swear I hear a faint hodgepodge of voices, but I can't be sure.

All of a sudden, large hands are on my body, holding me from what feels like every angle, and I'm being lifted away from the tub.

Coughing and spluttering, I try to suck in deep lungfuls of air as I'm forced upright and cradled against a massive chest. A towel is tightly wrapped across my back and shoulders and I realize I'm shivering uncontrollably. Through the ringing in my ears, I hear Stu's calming voice behind me. Tears leak from my eyes as my head pounds and the intensity of the situation I was just in comes crashing down around me.

I inhale deeply, the scent of coffee and whiskey fills my nose and I jolt in realization. That was the scent that surrounded Alpha...*Charlie.*

"You ok, baby?" His thick voice causes tingles to tangle within my body...and my core.

"Y-yes," I murmur. "Th-thank you." I'm still shivering, still scared, and kind of mad that I couldn't even clean myself without causing a scene. *Idiota.*

"Bea, do you want me to help you finish?" Stu's voice is soft and runs over me like a comforting blanket. I nod silently, completely abashed by my circumstances. But, thankfully, neither of them comment. Instead, some kind of silent dance begins. Charlie squats low, squeezes me to his body, and dips my head back while Stu tenderly rinses my hair out.

It's so sweet, so amazing...so disarming.

After he's finished, Charlie grunts and the water turns off. Stu begins to lightly dry my hair with another towel and his face comes into view as he prods the, most definitely, swollen lump on the top of my head.

"No bleeding, and it's swelling outward so, that's good." I can't tell if he's talking to me or himself so I just take in his features.

His crazy piercings, sparkling eyes, and tousled hair make him look like a bad boy. However, his charming smile, and all-around silly nature, prove he's anything but. *Dang, he's pretty.*

Charlie chuckles, causing my body to jump repeatedly from the movement and Stu smiles wide, his eyes sparkling with sheer joy.

"I, uh, I didn't mean to say that out loud." My whole body flushes and I find myself snuggling further into Charlie, hoping to make myself invisible.

Alas, it doesn't work.

"You're prettier, Queenie," Stu says with a little playfulness in his voice. My body flushes harder before he tugs a little in my hair.

Thankfully, they put me out of my misery.

Charlie carries me down the hall and sets me down on the bed. Stu follows closely behind with my clothes and brush.

He lays everything on the bed next to me as I work to make sure my body is totally covered by the towel. Thankfully, they are all pretty big dudes so they have the extra-large towels.

They both head for the door and I can't help but watch them walking away. Charlie looks back briefly, seeming a little irritated, but not as much as before so, progress.

Stu, on the other hand, gives me the widest, most beautiful smile and I find myself mirroring it.

"When you're done, join us in the kitchen. It's Even's turn to make dinner and I hear Danny talked him into his famous Chicken Piccata. It's *muah*," he makes the finger sign for chef's kiss and "throws it in the air." Again, I can't help but smile at his antics.

With a silent nod, I agree and wait for them to leave before struggling with putting my bra on. I finally manage to get the hooks clasped; or, at least, most of them. Deciding it's good enough, I slip on a loose black shirt that reads "Easily distracted by books" and I'm suddenly a little sad that I don't have any to help me pass the time.

I slide on a pair of shorts, knowing they will be infinitely easier to get on than jeans and turn to the dresser to swipe my hairbrush.

Once I'm, sort of, put together, I hobble down the hallway and hang up the towel on the towel rack. Then, I turn in the opposite direction and move past the room I've been staying in for the very first time.

CHAPTER 17

Charlie

We're all huddled around the table, the subtle hint of lemon butter wafting through the air. The image of *Franco Guillero* is pulled up on my laptop. Smug lookin' bastard would make a good Abercrombie model. He's annoyingly good-looking; no facial hair, a chiseled jaw, a slightly crooked nose, and that whole "beach blonde" combover that was popular in the early 2000s.

Based on the information Stu gathered, he was in and out of foster care after his Mom overdosed on heroin when he was 5. He dropped out of high school his freshman year, then started working for local gangbangers.

Apparently, Franco here has been noticed by all the right people and quickly moved through the ranks of the Crimson Knights. He was last photographed at the Baker's Rack- a local Hookah lounge and bakery. They also, allegedly, dabble in some not-so-legal sales in the back room. *Seems like a good place to go undercover.*

Just then, the smell of lavender and eucalyptus envelop me. *This woman here...*

I suck in a deep breath and count backward from ten so I can recenter myself. I swear I'm trying to keep my distance but she calls out to the possessive, protector in me. *The Omega to my Alpha.*

"Oh! Franco! How do you know him?" The entire atmosphere stills and immediately fills with tension.

Turning around, I see that the little vixen taking up residence in my home, and in my head, is crouched behind me. Her hair is artfully messy, still a little wet, and she has on a baggy black shirt with books outlined in the middle of it. However, I can't see more than that because the gentle curve of her breasts pressed against the shirt catches my complete attention. *'Cause, you know, I'm apparently a teenager around her.*

Thankfully, Even's brain is still functioning, so he asks the important question. "How do you know Franco?"

Her face tinges bright pink as she stands to her full height. But then, we all watch in awe as she straightens, rolls her shoulders back, and tips her chin in the air like the mini-badass she is. "A friend."

"Friend?" Stu blurts; anger mixed with disbelief. He swore she really didn't have friends. So, what are the odds she's actually been "casually hanging out" with a member of the Crimson Knights?

"Why does it matter? Who I spend my time with is none of your business. Unless, of course, you're trying to trick me into another gang bang."

I shoot a look to Stu, who is sitting to my left, directly in my line of sight. The hurt and guilt filling his eyes makes me lose it.

With a growl, I slam my hands on the table, shove the chair back, and whirl on Beatrice. I vaguely see that the others are also moving to intervene, but I would never, *ever*, hurt a woman.

I eat up the distance she put between us when I flung my chair backward. Raising a finger, I tower over her and point right at her nose. "Listen here, little girl," I spit. I shake my head at the audacity of this woman making Stu, and probably Even, feel like shit; again.

"You can be pissed all you want but they did nothing wrong. You meet Even on a fucking app-"

"That's bullcrap." She starts but I just keep going.

"You told Even your little fantasy and guess what? He just so happened to know a group of guys more than willing to make your fantasy come true. Whether we knew you before or not is completely irrelevant because at the end of the da-"

"They lied! I didn't know! It's still a lie by ommissio-"

"No! At the end of the day, you said "yes". Repeatedly. *You* didn't have to let us touch you. You didn't *have* to share about your intimacy issues with aftercare. You didn't have to admit you fell in love with *Stu*."

I see her eyes widen and flick over to Stu; as if she had already forgotten that she not only admitted it out loud, but she also wrote it in a fucking suicide note. *Which reminds me...*

"And what the hell are you so mad about anyway? You were going to run off and *kill yourself* after our night together. You were leaving *forever*, yet you didn't even bother to tell your *best friend*? The man you supposedly loved? I mean, what kind of bitter, selfish person does that?!"

"Enough!" Danny yells, snapping me out of my rage. I blink a few times, slowly returning to the here and now, forcing me out of the rant I've secretly told Cammy's ghost a million times in the dead of night.

Beatrice is a blur in front of me, but thankfully after a few more blinks, her normal form appears. Her face is twisted in agonizing pain, heartache, guilt, fucking everything awful.

And I did that.

I roughly rub a hand up and down my face and step away from her. After a few passes around the kitchen island, I come to a stop in front of the three men who are like family, and the one woman who I can't help but wish was.

"I-I'm sorry." My hands shake as I clench them into fists. The guys are wearing various expressions of understanding, anger, and shock. I've never yelled at a woman like that before. Hell, I rarely unload on the guys like that.

Glancing up at Beatrice, I see that her mask of indifference and anger is firmly back in place.

Then something happens. Something I sure as shit didn't have on my Bingo card for this woman.

"No." She asserts calmly. Her shoulders just barely curve inward and tears openly stream down her beautiful, fucking face. Looking me dead in the eye, she nods her head subtly.

"No. Do not say "sorry". Because," she sighs heavily and I see the walls built up around her slowly start to crack.

She slowly starts to crack.

"Because you're right. You don't know, they don't know," she waves her hand toward Danny and Even, standing off to the right of the kitchen table.

"My life..." Shaking her head vigorously, she stares down at the table, like she's trying to find the words.

Clearing her throat, again, she looks back at me, tilting her head just so, and says, "My life has been a series of terrifying events. Attack, after attack, after attack. My body has been taken against my will more times than I care to remember. It's also been beaten more times than I want to remember. I've been manipulated, broken, and torn down so many times, that I just couldn't do it anymore. I couldn't take it.

I, um, I like Even. A lot. And, you, Alpha...Charlie... I was falling for you, too. Then, when I met Danny, I had a strange connection with him. Like, like..."

She trails off. Danny, bouncing on the balls of his feet, blurts out excitedly. "Magic! It was pure magic. I felt it, too, Flower." His smile takes over his entire face, making him look absolutely insane. *And, honestly, kind of adorable.*

She chuffs a laugh, and shakes her head as she rolls her eyes. She tries to hide her smile, but it's definitely there. I can tell by the way her eyes brighten and the lines above her mouth move, making the heart shape of her face more pronounced.

"Anyway," she continues, again. "I was overwhelmed. I don't *do* feelings, I don't *do* relationships, and I certainly don't do *intimacy.* Hence, the rules, the apps... I just. I can't survive being hurt again. I just, I can't."

"But you did," Stu says, breaking his silence for the first time. Tears are flooding his face, and his eyes and nose are red-rimmed, but there's a steely determination in his eyes.

"Wh-what?" She stammers.

"You did survive being hurt again. You slid your bike into a guardrail and fell 30 feet down an embankment. Hell, Bea, some of the witnesses say you didn't fall, you fucking flew! And guess what, you're here. Hurt? Yes. In some pain? Also yes. But, like the badass that you fucking are, you survived!"

He shuffles forward, coming to a stand right in front of her, before gradually sliding his hands onto her cheeks. His thumbs rub away her tears and I can't help but wish that was me. *I want to comfort her. I want to calm her.* Fuck, *I want to hold her.*

Stu's voice lowers, but the silence in the house allows his voice to travel just enough that we can hear every word. "I hate what's happened to you, Bea. All the things you told me, all the things you didn't. But those things, Beatrice, those things make you the woman you are. You may be scared to feel, worried to fall, but guess what? We're here to catch you. *I'm* here to catch you." He leans in until he's just a breath away.

"Besides, no other woman takes on the scumbags who get away with trafficking, with rape, with hurting innocent children... *You* do that, Beatrice. You! And, dammit, I fucking love you."

His mouth immediately slams into hers, almost knocking her over. Her back goes ramrod straight for all of two seconds before she lets go. Before she *allows* herself to let go.

And, by God, it's glorious.

CHAPTER 18

Holy cannoli! This kiss! This dang kiss is...everything! His tongue plunges into my mouth. He's not hoping, praying, or requesting. Oh no...Stu is demanding, owning, claiming. *Fork nuggets it's hot!*

For a brief moment of time, I let his words sink in. I open myself up to the possibility of this, of us, and I let myself feel.

Before I know it, he's releasing my mouth, then coming back for a nip, a peck, and then another sweet, chaste kiss before he smiles that darn, dimpled smile, and I swear to you, I friggin' swoon.

Then, with his hands still on my face, his face slowly transforms into something firm, more serious. "No running, Bea. It's you and me, now. I'm not asking. We're past that, now. Ok?"

I blink, stunned completely stupid, as his words settle into the marrow of my bones. Then, reality crashes down on me. The air backs up in my lungs and I feel my eyes widen to the size of tea saucers.

"Whatever's spinning on that hamster wheel in your head, stop. We all want you, even the grumpy brute. You can choose to be with any, or none of us. You don't even have to decide now. In fact, I'd like to take you on a date. Where do you wanna go? Name the place! Ooo, do you like seafood? I know this great place on the water-"

"Danny, shut it!" Even snaps.

And, I can't help it, I bust out laughing. Dang it all. He's so forkin' cute. No wonder Even loves him. *Wait, Even...*

My eyes snap toward Even and I implore him to forgive me. His boyfriend literally just asked me on a date in front of him. Oh my God! *I've been here for less than two weeks and I'm already causing issues. Crap, crap, crap.*

Even's sexy-as-sin grin slowly grows across his face and he steps forward. Stu's hands are mysteriously missing from my face; which I realize only because I can turn to face Even fully, without restrictions.

He comes to a stop right in front of me but makes no move to touch me. His smile widens and good gracious, this sexy Viking of a man really is delicious. I have the overwhelming urge to reach out and rub his beard, wondering if it's as soft as it looks.

I'm grateful as he takes that moment to interrupt the intrusive thoughts. "I, too, am interested. I have been since the first time we messaged through the app, and it's only grown since then. I would also like to get to know you better, barring your normal "rules". I want this. I want you both." He shares with a huge smile, turning to look behind him at Danny. Danny's answering grin and, not-so-subtle nod, are all he needed.

Or, all *we* needed, maybe.

Clearing my throat, I swipe the last few errant tears away from my face before looking at Charlie. Then, Stu, Danny, and Even. Chewing on my lip, I try to consider the good, the bad, the ugly, the forking painful...but at the end of it, Stu's right. I have freaking survived. A lot. So, maybe I can have some fun, and possibly, a little bit of hope.

"So, uh, you all, what? Wanna share me? Like a poly relationship or reverse harem or something?"

Naturally, Danny is the first to speak up. "Yup. Just like your books! We're good boys. We know how to share."

Stu chortles and Even just shakes his head, clearly exasperated with his boyfriend.

"Wait, my books?" I shriek.

Danny's smile turns a little guilty, a little bashful, as he admits, "Uh, yeah. There were some books on your dresser, and they sounded kind of cool so I, um, borrowed them?" He shrugs and blushes a little.

I can't even be mad he took them without asking. If anything, I'm glad I have some books here now. So, I smile at him and playfully shrug, "Well, I guess that means we're going to have to form our own book club."

He perks up instantly, the light shining in his eyes again, and nods adamantly.

Finally, I step away from Even with a soft smile and shuffle to stand a few feet in front of Charlie. With a deep, almost exhausted breath, I gaze up at him.

It feels like a whole lifetime of conversations passes through our eyes before I inhale deeply and express, "Listen, I know you don't like me-"

"No, please. No." He abruptly cuts me off, stepping closer to me with his hands out in a sign of peace. "I do. I do like you, Beatrice. My little Omega. I have since our first video chat, and I haven't wanted anyone in, well, um, years. Like the others, we can take it slow. We'll each have our own time with you if you want. If you decide one, or more, of us would be better as just friends, really, truly just friends, and not because you're scared, then we'll deal with it. We're all grown-ups. We all want to be part of your life and to have you part of ours. Okay?"

His whole spiel makes a whole kaleidoscope of butterflies take off in my stomach.

Yes, that's really what a group of butterflies is called. Another random fact I learned for no reason at all. *I wonder if they'll think my quirks are cute, or annoying. Like, knowing that a pack of crows is called a murder of crows. See, weird, random, mostly useless.*

Backing away from my intrusive thoughts, I smile back at him, almost shyly, and reach my hand out. I figure a man who relates to Alphas in fantasy books would appreciate a hand-shake over a hug. His brows furrow into a deep v as he regards my hand. Looking between my eyes, and my hand, he starts to chuckle before placing his in mine and shaking it. Like, we're shaking on a deal.

It's weird, goofy, but it feels oddly right.

Clearing his throat behind me, Stu slides a hand down my arm until it connects with my left hand before tugging me away. "So, Queen Bea, tell us all about Franco."

Well, here's to hoping this cracked foundation isn't about to crumble.

Lord help me, now.

~CHAPTER 19~

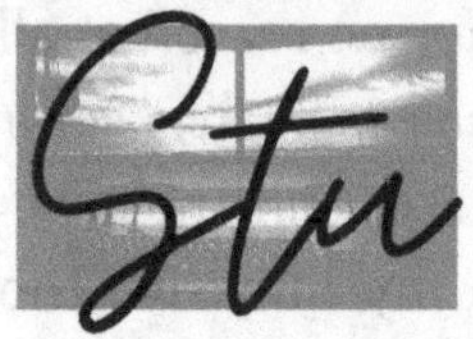

I help Bea get situated in the chair by the laptop and pull another one over so she can prop up her leg. She smiles shyly and I swear my heart flips. *Did that really just happen? Did she really let me kiss her and agree to give us a chance?*

Even brings over a pillow, lightly nudging me out of the way so he can slide it under her leg. We all take our places around the table before the strangest sound erupts from Bea's direction.

Her face turns a hilarious shade of crimson and she bows her head to hide. Charlie, the moody bastard, grunts, "When was the last time you ate?"

For an awkward moment, we wait for her answer. Or should I say, Danny, Even, and I wait. Charlie's already making his way back into the pantry and rummaging around. Her face tilts as she tries to see what he's doing. "Um, I don't remember."

Even speaks up, "And your meds? You can't take those on an empty stomach."

Her brows pinch in concentration but that's telling enough as is. Danny hops up and rushes down the hall to grab her medicine.

By the time he returns, Charlie's placing a bottle of water in front of her. She uncaps it and I watch as she takes a few gulps. Then, she pops the pills into her mouth, takes another swig of water, and swallows them down. *How does she make taking medicine sexy? Jesus.*

Clearing her throat, she watches as Danny slides into a chair next to Even; across the table from her. I'm sitting to her right so her back is slightly turned toward me so she can use the chair in front of her for her left leg.

"So, uh. How much do you want to know?" Her inquiry sounds serious, but there's something hidden in it.

"Everything." Charlie's gruff, no-nonsense voice carries from the kitchen island.

Her head tilts and I can tell by the straightening of her shoulders, and the slight wave of her hand, that my Sassy Queen is getting ready to come out.

"You sure about that? Because, you may not like what I have to say." Her voice is strong, challenging. Fuck, I love it. *That's my girl.*

Charlie stops what he's doing and glares at her under his lashes. "Yes, little girl, I am." *Oh hot damn.* Dominant Charlie has come out to play.

I can see the blush forming on Bea's cheeks and I can't help the small grin that forms.

Danny's rocking back and forth on the back legs of the chair and Even's chest is rising and falling in a staccato rhythm from holding in his laugh.

"Ok. You asked for it." Her playful reply, and the smile I see form across her face, force me to reach over and grab her hand.

At first, she clenches at the contact, and stares at our joined hands like they may jump up and bite her. Eventually, after some kind of internal debate, she takes in a deep breath and lets it out slowly.

Turning a little more, she looks over at me and gives me a smile that lights up the whole damn world. *She's trusting me. Allowing herself to be vulnerable, and damn it feels fucking amazing!*

Clearing her throat again, she looks between us and begins, "So, Franco and I met through the same app we met on." She gestures to Even and I see his face fall; likely knowing where this is going.

Danny's front chair legs slam to the ground as he shifts forward. "Why would he need to use the app? I mean, the Crimson Knights are crawling with molls and wannabes. Why use an app?"

Beatrice glances at Even, then back to Danny, before answering. "Well, I guess he didn't want the others to know what he had going on."

She's purposefully leaving out information. Looking around, I can tell I'm not the only one confused.

"Ugh, fine," she growls out, tipping her head back toward the ceiling, and shaking it a few times. She releases a heavy breath before rambling out, "He has a micropenis. A lot of men have hard times, socially, sexually, and emotionally. He told me he doesn't seek out those around him because he doesn't want to be chastised. Men and their dicks." She grumbles the last part under her breath and rolls her eyes.

The entire kitchen is eerily silent. Even Charlie is frozen over the plate of food he's been preparing for Bea.

Danny, being Danny, braces his arms on the table, clasps his hands, and leans forward; as if he's sharing a secret. "So, um..."

His eyes sparkle with mischief and I can already tell what he's going to ask.

"How was it?"

She snaps her head towards his in surprise and guffaws. "Fine. He was fine. We met up twice and it was fine."

"So, he didn't get you off but you're still trying to be nice?" Charlie and his damn mouth.

Before I can say anything, she whips her head towards him and glares. "I understand conditions out of our control. I have two, both preventing me from always crossing the, uh, the line. You know..." She trails off flitting her hand through the air like it's magically going to speak for her.

"An orgasm, little girl? It's hard for you to orgasm?" Her hand stops mid-air and her eyes widen. A deep, sexy blush trails from her ears, across her face, and down her neck.

I reposition my body as my cock stirs to life.

"Y-yes. Actually. Sometimes I do, sometimes I don't. And, that's ok. Doesn't mean he wasn't friggin' amazing with his fingers." She may have started off with stammering, but she quickly gained confidence. And I know I'm not the only one who caught the challenge in her voice on the last statement.

Charlie growls in his chest and Even wipes a paw down his face, stroking his beard a few times. "Listen," she laments, "It was fine. He was fine, but other than that, we didn't share much personally. A couple of meetings, one was in the back of a bakery or something, and then, yeah, we parted ways." She shrugs a shoulder like it's no big deal but holy shit!

Charlie's frozen where he stands and appears to be piecing through what she's told us.

Shaking his head, he walks over and sets down a plate with a giant club sandwich piled high with lettuce, tomato, turkey, and ham. I'm not even sure he remembered he was making it for her and not himself because it's twice the size of her mouth.

Her eyes grow wide and she murmurs a soft, "Thank you," before picking up a triangle, squishing it down a little, and taking a bite.

To my great surprise, she actually fits the sandwich in her mouth and moans. Telling by the off-orange sauce dabbed at the end of her mouth, he added his special chipotle mayo to the sandwich.

My cock jumps in my sweats and I hear Danny and Even both groan.

Her eyes pop open as she covers her mouth with one hand and wipes the side of her mouth. Taking a moment to chew, she looks at Charlie and tells him, "This is forking AMAZING!"

Charlie looks almost bashful as he grunts, "Dinner won't be for another hour, and you need all the nutrients you can get so, yeah. No big deal." He quickly turns away and begins putting up the rest of the food.

Bea finishes chewing another bite of her sandwich before looking around, "So, why do you need to know about Franco?"

Naturally, we all look to Charlie for direction. A few beats pass as he continues cleaning before he responds. He comes to a stand on the closest side of the island, leans against it, and crosses his arms over his chest.

I hold my breath, completely unsure of how this is going to be handled, but leave it to Charlie to make the right decisions.

"I'll tell you what. We'll tell you what our business with Franco is, given our boss approves, if you tell us why you have a dungeon below your garage."

Bea's hands start trembling as she gently places the sandwich on her plate. Dropping her chin to her chest, she takes a few calming breaths.

Leaning over, I squeeze her thigh, silently lending my support. Her head slowly turns to face me and I give her, what I hope, is an encouraging smile. "You can trust them. In fact, it will all make much more sense if we all work together." I whisper the words just for her to hear before leaning in and giving her a chaste kiss.

Opening her eyes, I see tears filling them and I tilt my head. "Only tell them what you're ready to share, but I guarantee there won't be any negative judgment."

With a small nod, she releases a shaky breath and waves Charlie to the table. "Can you, um, please sit? I might be able to get through this if no one's standing above me."

Charlie sees it in her eyes, I know he does.

He nods once and slides into the chair at the end of the table. She meets each of our eyes, assessing our seriousness and, I'm sure, warring with herself about being vulnerable.

"Before you decide to "date me", or whatever," she uses air quotes and I roll my eyes. *Like I could possibly leave her.*

"There are things you need to know. Since there are four of you and one of me, I can't explain the dungeon without explaining my 'why'."

Charlie nods solemnly, Even's nervously stroking his beard, and Danny looks an awful lot like he's walking a tightrope with his beast.

Staring into my eyes once more, she smiles, mouths "thank you", and begins.

~CHAPTER 20~

After Beatrice spent almost a full hour pouring out her fucking soul, I headed to our gym for some cleansing.

That fucking woman. While she didn't go into great detail, she shared enough. Well, too much.

She's gone through far fucking too much and it pisses me off to no end. Some stories she cried, some she glossed over like "it is what it is", and some she stared off into space like she was telling someone else's story; like she had to disassociate from the story just to get through.

But then, oh, and then...she took every one of those assholes out. Realizing how Stu was helping was only partially surprising. Of course, we knew he'd only help if their morals aligned. Stu may have a bleeding heart, but his moral compass is firmly intact.

She was so exhausted, her pain meds pulling her down during the last fifteen minutes or so, that Stu gathered her into his arms and tucked her in bed.

The kitchen was completely silent while Beatrice ripped her heart out and handed it straight to us. Little does she know, she's ours now; whether she likes it or not.

By the time Stu returned, we had migrated to the living room. He plopped onto the couch and blew out a heavy breath. After five minutes of staring at the spot Beatrice had been sitting on, I stood and walked out of the living room without a backward glance.

Now, I'm wrapping my hands, ready to attack the shit out of the heavy bag so I can push my beast back. He's been roaring his ugly head since Bea's first admission; mainly because the thought of another man touching her makes me irrationally jealous.

But then, her tenacity, her strength, her goddamn audacity to seek vengeance and rise above her traumas. *All* of them.

Jesus, she's amazing!

Once my hands are wrapped, I whip off my shirt, leave my basketball shorts on, and head to the speaker system we have set up. Pairing my phone, I click on Ronald by Falling in Reverse. It's the only song that matches the war raging in my head; and it hits fucking hard.

Squaring up to the bag, I roll my shoulders, then let loose.

I let out all of my aggression, all of my jealousy, all of my feelings of hopelessness and anger; wondering why. Why has this woman been put through the wringer time and time again? What was the point?

My beast rages with the need for vengeance, even though I know damn well that she took care of each and every one of the bastards. Warmth rushes through my veins with each swing, each punch, each connection with the bag. I need to irradicate my demons so I can be the man Bea deserves, one she desires, one she never, ever has to regret being vulnerable with.

Within ten minutes, my body quakes from over-exertion. I know I shouldn't haul off like that, but I needed it. I needed to do it or I'd end up making some stupid ass mistake like handcuffing her to the bed and making sure nothing bad ever happens to her again.

Now that I'm stretched out on the mat, panting heavily and dripping sweat, I vow to ensure nothing bad happens to her, again. Luckily for her, I've at least let go of the idea of holding her hostage for the rest of our lives.

A cool, wet cloth slaps onto my face, causing me to gasp and sputter in surprise. "The fuck?" I roar, popping up to stand while ripping the cloth from my face.

Charlie stands at the doorway of the gym, leaning against the doorjamb with his arms crossed over his chest. "You alright?" He drawls with that growly voice of his.

"Yeah. Better." I pant out, still perturbed that he hit me with a cold rag.

He tilts his head and assesses me. The man knows just how to read me so there's no point in lying. And, yeah, I'm better.

Seemingly satisfied, he lifts off the doorjamb and takes a step back. "Living room in ten. Just got off the phone with HQ."

My blood turns cold. If HQ doesn't let us bring her into the fold, she'll close right back up. I just know it.

With a stiff nod, he retreats and makes his way back down the hall. I take in a few controlled breaths, closing my eyes and hoping for a good outcome. I'm not even sure what we would do if this doesn't work out like we hope, but I guess I'll learn soon enough.

I jog over to the counter where our mini-fridge is, and down half a bottle of water. Re-capping it, I turn and make my way to my room.

I need a good shower, and maybe a firm tug on my dick to prepare for this conversation.

~CHAPTER 21~

Even

I'm sitting on the bed, waiting for Danny to get out of the shower. My hands are bunched in my hair and my elbows are resting on my knees. *Fuck.*

Beatrice is everything I hoped she was, thought she was, and so fucking much more. In fact, she did nothing but cement how perfect she was for me, for us.

Damn, I really hope she's still serious about us dating her because, honestly, I need her. We all do.

Danny steps out of the bathroom, a light blue henley stretching across the lean muscle bunching underneath the fabric. The bastard gives me a smug grin, likely having caught me checking him out. But, hey, he's mine. I can look all I want.

"Ready?" He asks almost morosely. With a nod, I take in a deep breath, closing my eyes, and releasing it. Once I open my eyes again, I find his hand near my face, offered out to me as a sign. Whatever happens, we'll deal with it like we do everything else; together.

With our hands linked, I let him pull me up and lead me out of the room, down the stairs, and to the living room.

Charlie's sitting in his favorite recliner. Stu's spread out across his; his left side propped up against the arm of the recliner and his legs hanging over the right side. I swear the guy has no clue how to relax like a normal person.

Danny and I take up our spots on the couch and turn to face Charlie. "Boss," I prompt.

Charlie meets each of our gazes for a brief moment before beginning.

"So, it took some finagling, but HQ ran Bea's info." I feel my brows hit my hairline, not expecting them to have done a full damn check in such a short amount of time. Especially if all we're doing is letting her know how dangerous Franco is.

"HQ wants Beatrice on file."

Danny jumps up with a roar of disbelief, "What!? Are you insane?"

Charlie leans back, nonplussed by Danny's outburst, and flops his head to the side; signaling for Danny to get it all out now.

"She's been through enough! And now you want to bring her on the team, put her front and center as a target? She's been through enough pain in her life. And, what? We're just going to set her up for more?"

Danny's pacing behind the couch. His breathing is coming out in harsh pants.

I'm just about to intervene when Charlie barks, "Enough!"

Danny freezes, his eyes widen to the size of saucers, and he angrily stares down Charlie. "By all means, oh wise one, do enlighten us." *Sassy fuck.*

Charlie groans and rolls his eyes before shifting his body forward, resting his elbows on his knees, and clasping his hands together tightly. "If she decides to join Vidar, she will automatically be placed on our team, not anyone else's. Additionally, they will allow her to skip normal training due to her, um, extra-curricular activities. However, she has to agree to work as a team, and, she can't go outside the lines."

He pauses long enough to give Stu a long look. "That means no more side projects." Stu nods solemnly and lets his head fall between his shoulders as he stares at the ceiling.

Eventually, Stu lifts his head and gazes at Charlie. "So, what now, Boss Man?"

"Now," Charlie sighs heavily, running a meaty hand along his jaw. "Now, we present it to her. If she doesn't agree, well, we can still...pursue her. However, we'll have to keep our professional lives, and any information about our jobs, completely private."

A heavy silence blankets the room. I mean, we know the score. We can't go around telling people what we do, but *how do we show her how serious we are if we can't come home and share things with her? How do we utilize our dungeon downstairs without being able to tell her why?*

That, and about twenty other questions filter through my mind. I'm assuming the others are thinking the same as we all sit in silence, with nothing more than our breathing to fill the space.

~CHAPTER 22~

I wake up a little groggy but feeling, oddly, light. Stu knew most of what I shared but not all. I could tell he struggled with not knowing all the details. They all did. But, I'm also relieved none of them pushed for more. By the time I was done, I was well and truly exhausted. I don't remember coming back to my room but judging by the view of the backyard, I somehow made it back.

My eyes snag on a tablet someone left behind. I live for music. In fact, my brain randomly sings at least once an hour while awake.

Not ready to face the guys after the info dump, I reach for the tablet and easily find the YouTube Music app. I giggle a little, seeing a list of the most recent plays and, whoever owns this tablet, is polyjamorous like I am. I like it.

Wanting to cleanse some of the overwhelming feelings flowing through my body, I click on Rhianna's Stay before clicking the tablet screen off and setting it back down on the nightstand.

Closing my eyes, I fall back against the bed, and let the lyrics flush my system.

Water drips down my cheeks and I take a stuttered breath knowing that I really need to let it all out.

I can't believe I actually agreed to date them. Four of them! Four, what? Four boyfriends? Man friends? *Ew, no.*

I won't lie, I'm shocked that they all *truly* want me. And, not just want me, they want to be with me. *Or so they say.*

Then, barely ten minutes later, I'm spilling my whole, trau-matic, jacked-up life. Unfortunately, the meds had me passing out before any of them could do anything other than sit there in silent shock and stare at me like I was a fragile pane of glass standing before them.

Now, I'm nervous. Will they still want me? Now that they know how broken, how damaged I am?

A soft knock on the door causes me to jump. Pulling up the blankets, I quickly run my fingers through my hair and call out, "C-come in."

Stu pokes his head in, his smile widening as he sees me awake. He looks like he's showered recently. His skin looks brighter, and his piercings reflect the soft light emitting from the ceiling lights.

"Hey, beautiful," I swear his smile grows and I can't help but smile back at him.

"Hey." Clearing my throat, I nervously look around, letting the soft side of my blanket ground me.

"Um, would you like to come in? I, uh, guess, maybe we should talk."

With a subtle nod, he squeezes in, not letting the door open all the way, before quietly clicking it shut.

He turns around, slips his shoes off, then crawls onto the bed. A tingle tangles through my body and I shift a little. He's so dang hot, it's unreal.

Sliding in next to me, he props himself up on his left elbow, turns onto his side, and looks down at me like I'm something precious, something important, something worthy.

"So...you sure you want this? With me I mean? I'm a hot mess. I hate being vulnerable, I haven't actually dated in, gosh, years, and I just, I don't know how to do thi-"

Suddenly, Stu's soft lips meet mine, effectively cutting my self-deprecating rant completely off.

This kiss isn't like the one we shared earlier, or almost two weeks ago. It's sweet, slow, explorative; like he's trying to memorize every bump, groove, and sound created by his long, delicious tongue.

The dance between our tongues is erotic, familiar, and I'm having a hard time telling my pussy to back the fork off.

Stu groans into my mouth, and before I can take my next breath, he's covering my body with his.

My legs spread to accommodate his size and I wrap my arms around his neck. Well, I do it as best as I can since I have a giant cast in my way. The good news is, Stu doesn't seem to be bothered about it. Instead, he continues his slow, passionate exploration of my mouth. With one arm propped near my head, he takes the one that was caressing my cheek and slides it down my body; lightly trailing his fingers down my collarbone, traveling over my breast, and continuing downward.

With deft fingers, he tickles the bottom of my top. Releasing me from our kiss, he stares down at me, those cool, blue eyes piercing deep into my psyche.

"Beatrice," My name sounds like a prayer and I know at the moment, I would gladly give this man everything he asks for.

"We should wait," His voice is laced with disappointment and resignation. And I can't help my response. The need pulsating through my body, soaking my panties, makes me want to have this moment with him. The moment I've been secretly dreaming about for years, but never allowed myself to hope for.

"Please, Stu. I need you." I thrust my hips up to meet his pelvis and he groans out.

He answers my plea with a thrust of his own and I curse the layers of fabric between us.

His mischievous grin, and glint in his eye, tell me that he not only isn't going to give me what I want, what I crave, but he's enjoying my predicament way too much.

I growl out, throwing my head back and rolling my eyes toward the ceiling. "Wh-hy?" I whine petulantly.

His answering chuckle lights my nerves on fire and my pussy clenches with need.

Bending down, he lightly kisses my nose and smiles down while saying, "Not yet, not like this. But, soon. Promise."

With a wink and another chaste kiss, his body heat disappears and I'm seconds away from throwing a full-body tantrum like a two-year-old.

"Jerkface," I mumble under my breath. His answering laughter follows him around the room as he slides off the bed, pushes his feet into his shoes, and heads for the door.

He turns to look at me over his shoulder, smirks, and says, "Naughty girl. I came to see if you're awake. Boss Man talked to HQ and has something to tell you." I narrow my eyes and glare at him because the laughter in his eyes means he's enjoying my little predicament all too much.

Reaching down, he not-so-subtly adjusts himself before winking at me. "You're not the only one Queen Bea. Now, get your beautiful ass up out of bed and come to the living room. Do you need help or you got it?"

"I've got it. Besides, I'm mad at you." I pout and am suddenly aware that I'm usually not this playful with others. It's nice, actually. He cackles and I throw a pillow at him.

And, just like before, he closes the door just before the pillow can connect and his laughter bounces down the hall as he walks away.

Ten minutes later, I've turned the tablet off, used the bathroom, brushed my teeth, and re-tied my hair up into a messy bun.

Stepping into the living room, I officially take in the surroundings. There's a battleship grey wall that the 70-inch TV sits against. The entertainment center is sleek, black, and boring, yet modern-looking. Strangely, it kind of matches the house. Greys and creams decorate the rest of the space, including the kitchen.

Two large maroon recliners sit diagonally towards the TV and are on opposite sides of a large, dark grey sectional that would easily fit 8 people. The strangest thing is the space still appears huge. Which, I mean, with four guys brooding around, I'm sure they need.

To my left, near the opening of the hallway I just walked out of, is a set of stairs. Just beyond that is a ginormous floor-to-ceiling sliding door overlooking the beautiful backyard. The front door appears to be on the other side of the living room, near another set of stairs. Geez, this place is massive.

The men in question begin walking into the living room with large trays of food and enough drinks to hydrate an army.

Charlie's face falls when he sees me and he freezes on sight. Danny almost runs into him and Even barely misses the backup by stepping around the other two. He, quite gracefully, trips, stumbles, dances around, then rights himself long enough to slide his huge tray of chicken piccata on the table. One lone caper bounces off the tray and he curses it out. "Stupid, piece of shit. You just couldn't stay on could ya? Trying to impress the pretty girl and you just had to dive-bomb the floor, didn't ya?"

I can't freakin' help it, I crack up laughing.

His head snaps toward me and I see his face pale enough behind his beautiful beard that I laugh harder. Charlie's still standing in the kitchen archway, seemingly dumbstruck, and Danny's cackling behind him.

Stu peers around Danny, raises a brow, and scans the room. Once he spots me, I see his cheeks lift with a smile. "Hey, beautiful! Fancy seeing you here."

Danny's eyes leak from laughter, causing me to crack up even harder.

After another minute, Danny and my laughter dies out and I watch as Stu shoves him aside, hands filled with beers, and swaggers over to me. His pink hair flops over his forehead as he approaches me. Then, he gives me the most toe-curling, drive-by kiss that leaves me reaching out for him as he cockily meanders over to the table to deposit the drinks.

Danny playfully shoves Charlie out of the way, which causes him to blink a few times before coughing a little and then moving briskly toward the table. Danny slides a tray filled with 10 different cheeses and a pile of strawberries dumped in the middle. Charlie's bowl is piled high with fettuccini. He steals a noodle, slurps it up, and swipes a beer before walking over to the far recliner and plopping into it.

Danny and Even grab a paper plate from a stack I hadn't noticed before, and pile them high with food.

Stu looks over at me and tilts his head. "Come on, Bea. Time to eat. I know you only ate half of your sandwich earlier. Tonight, we're having a movie and picnic night. Whatcha' want on your plate?"

Danny pops up quickly from where he was bent over the table and declares, "I've got it! I already loaded you up. Pretty flowers need their vitamins and plenty of energy." He smiles so wide I can't tell if it's cute or creepy, but his eyes gleam with excitement so I return his smile with a murmured, "Thank you."

Even piles up another plate of food, passes it to Danny, and the two of them sit on the end of the sectional furthest away from Charlie. Stu makes a plate before plopping into the remaining recliner; stretching out across the arms instead of using the actual footrest.

I stand there, awkwardly for a moment, before Danny pats the huge area of the sectional next to him. Tipping my lips in a small smirk, I put my head down and quickly make my way over to sit just as Charlie clears his throat.

"Please, eat. And, um, before we turn on the movie, we have an offer for you." I look between him and the others, trying to gauge their reactions, or any hint of what they may be about to drop in my lap. Unfortunately, they're all very good at wearing masks of indifference and my anxiety ratchets up.

"O-Ok." I stutter, nodding my head in acquiescence.

For the next fifteen minutes, Charlie explains the phone call he had with HQ. I'm given strict instructions to think about it, not give an immediate decision, before Danny pushes play on *Couple's Retreat.*

And for the next two hours, I don't think about my answer; or my predicament. For once, I sit back, enjoy my food with amazing, hot, funny, smart men, and lose myself in the hilarity that is Vince Vaugh and Jon Favreau.

~CHAPTER 23~

It's been two days since the Vidar Mercenaries officially offered me a job. Honestly, I had completely forgotten that I had quit my old job. Heck, I hadn't realized I had been without a phone because I spent my first week here in and out of consciousness and moping when I was awake.

I can't even begin to explain how strange the whole thing sounded. I mean, *mercenaries!* Real, vigilante groups hired by higher-up officials when the government ties their hands?! It's like something out of one of my books.

Charlie bought me a new phone with their numbers, and HQ's number already programmed. My first directive was to call HQ, listen to their spiel, and sign about a hundred NDAs and "other" documents. Thankfully, with my permission, they've put me on the guys' team so we don't have to hide things from each other; and I get to stay in this area.

I told Stu they knew he was helping me and looked so cute and bashful when HQ told me this was a warning. No more off-the-books vigilante-ism for us. I didn't have a problem with it since I'd already gotten my revenge. That, and, neither Stu nor I would get into actual trouble; this time.

Doc just left and he's pleased with my progress. Getting help washing my hair has still been a pain in the rear, but Stu and Danny are always around to help.

The guys were hilariously vocal about their *actual* feelings toward Franco and me having "relations". I rolled my eyes at their posturing and even chuckled at their disgusted faces.

After a couple of minutes, I was able to finally get us back on track by talking about the bakery he took me to; what I saw, who...

They literally asked a hundred questions until my head was spinning.

It appears that my random meet-up proved to be beneficial to a huge case they've been floundering with.

Now, I'm hobbling down the hall making my way to the kitchen. One thing I've loved about staying here is the amount of food these giants consume, and, therefore, have on hand. The pantry, fridge, and freezer are always packed to the gills with just about anything and everything you could possibly desire.

Opening the fridge, I find a new stack of cheese and cracker packs. They are my favorite and I briefly wonder who else enjoys them.

Grabbing one, I waddle over to the couch, and flip on the TV, quickly deciding to watch *The Naked Truth*. Charlie, Even, and Danny are out snooping around the bakery, and Stu is upstairs running codes on codes on codes. I knew he was smart, but holy crackerjacks! The things he can do with those long, lean fingers and a laptop is insanity.

Footsteps bounding down the stairs cause me to smile, ready to see the mop of pink hair sitting above the cutest smile ever.

Jumping down the last two steps, Stu lands on the floor with a *thump* before turning that heart-stopping grin on me. "Hello, there, Queen Bea. How are you feeling today? Need any help washing today?"

"Hey! No, thanks. Danny helped me wash my hair before they left this morning."

With a cocky little grin, he swaggers over to me before leaning down in front of me. He rests his hands on the back of the couch on either side of my head and stops just short of our noses touching. "I never said anything about washing your hair." He waggles his eyebrows before closing the distance and planting a toe-curling kiss on my lips.

I greedily open for him, maneuvering my legs to make room for his body. He slides one hand over my cheek and the other through my hair, tilting my head just so, and then proceeds to consume me wholly.

Suddenly, his hands leave my head. I feel one arm band around my back, and the other band underneath my huge behind. Then, I'm being lifted in the air.

I yelp out, clenching my arms around his neck. "Stop!" I screech. "I'm too heavy! Put me down." My anxiety spikes as I imagine us both crashing to the floor and me breaking every bone in his body.

A firm slap to my ass causes me to squeak in surprise and I realize that he's growling. Actually growling! "Don't you dare talk about my Queen's body like that. I won't stand for it. Now, hold on tight, I'm taking you back to your room."

I gawk at him in surprise; his firm voice sending tingles straight to my core.

Then, his lips slam into mine with fervor, stripping me of any coherent thought.

Before I know it, I'm being laid, ever so gently, on top of the bed I've been staying in. He leans back just long enough to rip his shirt off, and I can't help but roam my fingers across his lean torso; watching in rapt fascination as his muscles tense beneath my touch.

Continuing my exploration, I reach all the way down to the navy sweatpants and my eyes widen with intrigue as his bulge strains underneath the fabric. *Crap on a cracker. I remember him feeling big in my hand, but Dear Lord he's huge!*

His chuckle catches my attention and brings my gaze back to his eyes. He looks at me with a mixture of hunger and sheer appreciation causing me to momentarily forget that he's between my thighs, preventing me from rubbing them together.

Leaning back in, he removes my hands from his waistband and intertwines his fingers with mine. His mouth captures mine in a soul-altering kiss. It's sweet, pure, and full of more emotion than I know how to handle. But, I try anyway. Dang, do I try; *for him.*

Letting go of one of my hands, I feel his hand travel down my chest, gently cupping my breast and teasing the area over my nipple. Needing more, more of him, I find myself thrusting against him and damning the fabric between us straight to hell.

With a moan, I take my free hand and rub it up and down his soft skin, only pausing briefly when his muscles lock up as my fingers trail over jagged scars. I want to know who the fork touched him so cruelly, but now's not the time. He'll tell me when he's ready.

Seeming to be on the same page, he grinds his pant-covered cock against my pussy, right where I need him most. "S-Stu. Please." I whine.

"I know. I've got you baby. I'm going to give you everything you need and more." Plunging his tongue back in my mouth, I get lost in the slow and tender dance we begin to share.

Without disconnecting our mouths, he reaches between us and deftly unbuttons my jean shorts before unceremoniously ripping them away from my body. I don't even have a moment to miss the sudden loss of his body when he returns and presses his weight against me.

"Beatrice. I-I've," His face twists in pain, sadness, and desire; causing my heart to dang near beat right out of my chest.

"I know, Stu. I know." Taking my casted hand, I run my fingers across his brows then trail down his cheeks, before settling my palm against his cheek. I watch as he closes his eyes and leans into my touch, and tears prick behind my eyelids.

After a deep breath, he opens his eyes, and slides off the bed. I try to steel my expression, my hurt, but he must sense it as his solemn face turns into a sly grin. Teasing his waistband with his thumbs, he slowly slides his pants down, bringing his briefs along with them. His cock springs out, bobbing up and down with each beat of his heart and I almost choke on my tongue.

He's got to be at least 9 inches long and has six barbells lining the underside of his hard cock, making the perfect Jacob's ladder. His long, lean fingers warp around his shaft and he pumps it once, drawing out a perfect bead of pre-cum.

I subconsciously lick my lips, desperately wanting to taste him. Which, is forking weird, because guys are such a-holes when getting blow jobs. That, and, I have an *awful* gag reflex. Trust me, it's not fun for anyone involved.

However, for Stu, I want to try. *Dang do I want to try.*

His throaty chuckle snaps my gaze back to his and I see that he's playing with that dang labret. My entire upper body is on fire and I'm starting to get nervous. *Shoot. What if I'm not good enough? What if I can't take him all? What if-*

"Whatever's running through your mind, baby, stop. It's just us, here. Just be here with me. Do you trust me?"

My head is already nodding before he even finishes his question because *I do.* I do trust him. With everything I have and everything I am, I trust him.

His smile is so sweet and loving as he gently climbs between my legs. Our lips connect again in a sensual dance and he freaking finally touches me where I crave him most. The contact causes me to jump with a yelp. He immediately soothes it as he slowly circles my clit with the slightest of pressure. I can feel my pussy clench down on nothing at all and know that I'm already embarrassingly wet for him.

He breaks the kiss, one arm landing next to my head, our foreheads touching, and begins to explore my slick folds. My hips thrust upward, desperate for more contact as his eyes pierce through mine.

When he finally plunges a long finger inside of me, I feel myself bare down on him and my eyes flutter closed.

He leisurely pumps in and out of me with his long finger. My legs fall open further, just in time for him to insert a second finger, stretching me even more. "God damn. You're so tight, baby. So damn tight but so damn wet."

With bleary eyes, I look at his face and see the muscles in his jaw tensing as he grits his teeth. *Pump, pump, pump, twist.*

My back bows off the bed and Stu takes that opportunity to kiss me along my neck, sucking on that sweet spot right between my neck and clavicle.

"Condom?" He pants out. His whole body vibrates as if he's barely holding back.

Shaking my head, far too close to the edge, I rasp, "I'm clean. Can't have kids."

His body tenses as his eyes shoot to mine with questions. Questions I'm not ready to have, yet. Instead, I reach up and pull his mouth down to mine, sucking his labret into my mouth as his groan ripples through my body.

Releasing our kiss, I feel the head of his cock nudging against my entrance, right where his fingers are. I close my eyes and take a deep breath through my nose, willing away the memories of the last time I had such a huge dick rammed into me.

"Open your eyes, Bea. I need to see you. I need to see you as I stretch your pussy with my cock." Obeying immediately, I begin to tremble; partly in fear and partly with anticipation as he removes his fingers and slides his tip through my wetness.

His tip breaches my entrance and I hiss at the burning stretch.

I'm no virgin, but what the guys don't know, is I've only had actual intercourse three times in the last four years. I've met plenty of guys through apps, but only let myself have sex twice before meeting Even. With every guy before him, I nixed intercourse, only relying on mouths and hands to do our work; and, of course, the occasional toy.

The head pushes in, causing me to arch off the bed, not sure if I want more or less. *Why is his head so big?? It's not going to fit.*

His chuckle brings me back to Earth and he leans closer to my ear, his warm breath gliding over my skin, causing goosebumps to erupt all over my body.

"It'll fit, baby. You can do it." His words aren't necessarily dirty but I groan all the same.

Pulling out a little, then pressing back in, he looks at me like I'm a rare gem. I swear I feel the cool metal press into my core and my breath backs up into my lungs.

"Breathe for me, baby. Come on. I have six barbells and you can take everyone. Now, count with me. You ready?" I wrap my arms around his neck, making sure my free arm lies on his neck, and the casted arm sits on top so I don't hurt him.

With a shaky nod, I push out a breath and lock my eyes on his. The metal pops past the resistance and he freezes. "One." I moan, my eyes rolling back in my head.

Slowly out, then in.

Pop.

"Two".

Stu's arm begins to shake violently as he moves his hand from his cock to my clit, rubbing it in smooth, slow circles. "Oh, oh, oh my God!"

Slowly out, dragging out the barbells, then in.

Pop.

"Threeeee!!!" I yell out as an orgasm forking bowls me over out of nowhere.

By the time I blink out of it, Stu's popping another barbell in. "F-Four," I groan long and low.

The piercings are rubbing up against places I've never felt before. And holy forkballs!

Out, then in.

Pop.

"F-five!"

He continues his ministrations on my clit as he pulls back out and slams all the friggin' way home.

"SIX!" Another orgasm rips through my core, down into my toes, and my eyes slam shut. There's a high possibility that my pussy now houses my heart as it beats out an almost painful rhythm. *Cheese and rice, Batman. He's ripping me apart in the most delicious way.*

Sweet, loving lips touch mine and I open my eyes to find Stu, now resting his body on mine, both arms bracketing my head; eyes unfocused and teeth grinding together. The vein in his neck pulsates with the effort it's taking him not to move.

Finally, my body melts into the bed. Rolling my hips upwards, I urge Stu to move. "Please." He lands a sweet kiss on my nose as he slowly pulls out, each and every bell leaving the comfort of my pussy before slowly sliding back in.

And then, he finds a rhythm.

It's terrifyingly slow, sweet, and all-around lovely. His hips roll as he enters me, pulls out, and re-enters. I drown in his beautiful blue eyes as he slowly starts to screw me. Although, I know better. This isn't screwing. This is... the *other* thing. The thing I've never done and I'm too much of a coward to say it.

So, instead, I close my eyes, rear forward, and kiss him with all I have. With all the emotions I'm feeling.

And he rocks into me until our bodies are sweating, my bra and shirt are sticking to my skin and I'm not totally sure where I end and he begins.

He rocks until sparks fill my vision. My legs wrap around his because I suddenly need every inch of him touching every inch of me; like I need my next breath.

He rocks until he finally lets go with the sexiest moan I've ever heard, spilling inside of me before collapsing on top of me.

And we stay like that: entangled with each other, sweaty and sated while I rub my hands through his sweaty, messy hair and breathe him in, *us in*, for what feels like the very first time.

~CHAPTER 24~

I'm so ready to be home! I finally convinced Charlie to let me take Beatrice on a date. Of course, we can't leave the property. It's only been three weeks since her accident and though she's doing much better, physical therapy is kickin' her ass.

She doesn't sleep nearly as much as she did, even a week ago, and spends more time out of her room than in.

We can all tell by how Stu and her look at each other, and always find ways to subtly brush up against each other, that their relationship is flourishing...and more. I'm not exactly jealous, but I'd love to just lean over and kiss her gorgeous face whenever I damn well please.

Soon, I remind myself. *Soon.*

Bright lights illuminate my little dungeon as Charlie hauls 'Ol-what's-his-name' over his shoulder. His heavy steps tromp through the basement until he unceremoniously dumps the man onto my steel Dooms Day table.

I clap my hands merrily at the thought of slicing and dicing this pathetic waste of space. But, first, my date.

Charlie and I quickly gag and bind the man- who's happily snoring from the drugs we injected him with. I was hoping the gag would muffle the sound but, unfortunately, it just makes it louder. The only snores I wish to hear are my Flower's. *Oh! Flowers! I should get her some.*

Charlie clears his throat before facing me. He must see it written all over my face that my mind is definitely not on the man passed out on the table. With a thick finger, he points at me and sternly reminds me, "No going off the property. It's too dangerous and she's still healing. And, be fucking careful with her!" He growls out the last bit as if I would dare hurt Beatrice. I mean, unless she wanted me to, of course.

But, whatever. His chastisement doesn't affect me so I rattle off an "Ay-Yi, Boss," saluting him with a wide smile.

He chuffs and shakes his head at me before jogging back up the stairs.

Patting Fuckface on the shoulder a few times, I talk to the man on my table as if he could possibly hear me. "Welp, I've got a hot date. Gotta go, buddy. See you later!"
And then, I'm rushing up the basement stairs, grabbing my keys, and bounding through the garage. Tonight is going to be perfect. I just know it.

It takes me a little longer at the store than I wanted but, I had a really hard time picking out flowers at the store. There are so many. I almost went with roses, but they're so cliché, and I have a sneaking suspension that Bea feels the same.

Unfortunately, they didn't sell cacti there, or I would have searched out the Queen of the Night. *I wonder if she understands the significance of her profile picture choice.*

Shaking my thoughts free, I stand, freshly showered in my best black button-up and dark jeans. The bouquet of Stargazer Lilies wrapped in ribbon is giving off the most heavenly scent and I really hope Beatrice likes them; I sure the hell do.

Knocking on her door, I wait with bated breath as I hear rummaging, then a muffled non-curse; *so cute.* Finally, the door flings open and Beatrice stands in front of me in a soft-looking, pale pink dress. The pink covers most of her chest in a classy way, but hugs her breasts to the point that I can't help but stare at them.

"Ahem." *Oops.* "My eyes are up here, Tiger." Her eyes twinkle with mischief and my cock starts to harden.

"I-I'm sorry. You just look....damn." There really are no words. Her pale pink sleeves are wide and flowy and almost hit her elbow. The bottom part of the dress flares out with horizontal, white, and pale pink stripes. She has the cutest, beige flat on her right foot- since she can't wear anything on the left. The view gives me a little spark of color from a tattoo I was unaware she had.

I don't have time to check it out right now because I can feel her glare cutting into my head.

Snapping my eyes back to hers, I'm relieved to find her smiling with a tinge of blush spread across her cheeks.

Suddenly remembering myself, I thrust the bouquet at her. "Here. Um. I didn't know what you like so..." I trail off, palming the back of my neck and looking anywhere but at her. *Why can't I just act normal?*

"Oh my gosh! I love them! Lilies are my favorite flowers! And look," I find myself drawn back to her; the excitement radiating from her is infectious in all the best ways. "Some are still closed! That always makes for the best bouquets! As they grow, I get to experience each new bloom... and it keeps the room they're in smelling amazing for so much longer. Thank you, Danny!"

She squeals and launches herself into my arms. I'm too shocked to move at first and find myself unable to remember how to hug.

But then, she squeezes her left arm around me and presses her warm, soft body against mine. My arms finally remember their manners and they wrap around her, pulling her tightly into a sweet embrace.

Releasing her is so damn difficult but, I do have a plan. *Much to everyone's surprise.*

Stepping back, she quickly lies the bouquet on the nightstand, then returns; hobbling gracefully in her cast with each step.

Holding out my hand, she smiles as she tentatively places hers against mine. Taking that as a good sign, I entwine our fingers and slowly lead her down the hallway.

"As you know, we can't leave the property. So, I planned a couple of things we can do here."

She nods silently and I briefly wonder if that's good or bad. But, I decide to keep going anyway; trying not to second-guess myself along the way.

Opening the back door, we step outside. Thankfully, we're in our, like, fifth summer in Texas. Even though Thanksgiving is a week away, it's a crisp 76°F.

"Oh wow!" She comments, sounding breathy and tempting. *Shit, snap out of Danny.*

Her gaze is riveted to the large cabana area to the left of the pool. It's just out of view from her window, and I don't think she's ever actually left the house, so I hope she likes it.

With a smile, I tug her forward, and gently help her get situated on the ginormous, white cushions. The cushions are basically the size, and shape, of our sectional; so we can all relax under the awning if we want to. However, instead of being high off the floor, they're low to the ground. A three-inch, wooden base holds them up.

She leans against one of the headrests and crosses her right leg over her left. With a contented sigh, she looks around the space. A tiny gasp leaves her mouth and I know she's noticed my little secret.

With a slight chuckle, I scoot over to the far end of the cushions, lean over, and roll over the giant cooler. Getting up on my knees, I open it up and start laying out all the things I bought for our picnic. And, ok, I may have gone overboard.

There's one of those coochie trays, or however you say it. I also grabbed a sandwich tray made with Hawaiian rolls, Funyuns, Doritos, Ridges, Cheetos, *and* Fritos with bean dip, French Onion Dip, and Ranch Dip. I also bought two trays for dessert! One has four different kinds of brownies, and the other has six different types of cookies. I'm very proud of myself.

Her soft giggle stops my movements and causes me to look over at her. *Holy fucking shit!* This is the Bea I fell for that night at the bar. Her smile is contagious and it completely transforms her face.

With another breathy laugh, she chortles, "Are the others joining us because, I may be a big girl, but there's no way I can eat all of this." I feel like she didn't comment on her size maliciously, so I let it go for now; instead focusing on her actual question.

"Well, I didn't know what you liked and there were so many options. It's actually one of the reasons the guys don't let me grocery shop. I can never make up my mind so I just get it all."

A self-deprecating chuckle leaves my mouth and I shrug indifferently. But, this woman sees right through me.

Her hand on mine has me whipping my head to look at her. Instead of bright and playful, her face is sweet and soft, and...*damn I want to kiss her. Is it too soon?*

In a low voice, she smiles and says, "It's so sweet and utterly perfect. Thank you, Danny." Her eyes hold me hostage and I recognize this moment for what it is. She's letting her walls down, being vulnerable, and fuck I want to do the same.

Leaning a little more toward her, I smile softly and whisper, "You deserve the best. And we will always make sure you get it."

I hadn't realized that I kept moving toward her while speaking. But, once the words are out of my mouth, our breaths mingle and her sweet scent envelops me.

I wait, and wait, and w-

Her lips tentatively seek mine out, and I almost die on the spot.

~CHAPTER 25~

I have no idea why I initiated such an intimate gesture with someone I barely know but... *it feels so friggin' right.*

His lips against mine are like the ying to my yang and I swear I feel a piece of my soul click into place.

It feels overwhelming, freeing, intoxicating.

With a moan I deepen the kiss, swiping my tongue across his lips before sucking his bottom lip into my mouth. He groans in response and I can't help but smile at my ability to rile him up.

Surging forward, I move to plunge my tongue into his mouth before he abruptly pulls away.

As embarrassment overcomes me, I feel my eyes widen with shock as I fight against the tears that threaten to fill my eyes.

"No, no, My Flower," He whispers sweetly, rubbing away an errant tear with his thumb and palming the back of my neck with his other hand. "I would love to kiss you all night long, but I promised you a date and, I think kissing happens when I drop you off at your door."

A giggle escapes me as my body floods with relief. *Dang, he's good.*

I lean over his lap, pushing my boobs out enough that I graze his chest as I reach for the furthest food item. A sexy growl vibrates through his body as I slowly return to my spot, still brushing up against him, with a little club sandwich tucked between my fingers. I send him a cheeky grin and wink right as I take a bite.

I suddenly can't focus on him as the sweet Hawaiian bread mixes with the honey ham and roasted turkey in the sandwich. A low moan escapes me and my eyes flutter almost orgasmically.

"Beatrice," Danny's feral growl is so not what I expected to hear from him. Not that I'm complaining; my panties are now wet.

"Y-yes?" My stuttered response is breathy and there's no dang way he doesn't catch the desire in it.

He grabs my wrist, just tight enough that I couldn't slip away if I tried, and brings my hand towards him. With a low rumble, he states, "If you don't stop with those types of noises, this entire picnic will go to waste because I'll have to run upstairs and beg Even to get me off."

He takes the rest of my sandwich and slides it off my fingers with his mouth; licking every crumb as he moves. "Mmmm, so tasty."

Holy. Forking. Shells. That should not have been so hot.

My pussy clenches tightly, and I whimper as he slowly moves away.

Clearing his throat, he turns around, grabs another sandwich, and hands it to me.

"Ok, first date question one: Favorite color." I smile so wide that my cheeks hurt and shake my head before allowing him to control the date he so beautifully orchestrated.

And, for the first time in a long time, I feel content. Happy. Completely at peace.

Danny only lasted fifteen minutes through our date-night conversation before he hopped up and began excitedly rubbing his hands together. "Ok, Flower. Time to move on to the next part."

His smile is infuriatingly adorable and I chuckle at his antics.

His hand reaches out for me and I slide mine into his, allowing him to carefully pull me up. Linking our hands together, he bounds off toward the house; forcing me to laugh as I hobble along behind him.

Butterflies gather in my belly as I consider the possibility that he's hoping to have sex with me. Biting my lip nervously, I realize that Stu is the only one I've allowed myself to be truly intimate within, well, a long freakin' time. Years!

Now that the others have made their own declarations about getting to know me, do they expect sex right away? *Crap. Am I ready for that? It took me years and a near-death experience to let my walls down with Stu.*

Danny releases my hand, forcing me back to reality. I was so lost in my head that I didn't realize we had made it back inside. Or that we're standing in front of a door I assumed was a storage closet in the kitchen. Danny's eyes are boring into mine and my cheeks flush with embarrassment.

"I, I'm sorry. I was in my head. Did you say something?" Of course, my blush deepens as his mouth tilts up into a playful grin.

He chortles, shaking his head, and looks at the door, then back at me. "No. Um, I want to show you something. Well, I want, um..." He trails off, releasing my hands and looking all kinds of bashful.

Wanting to put the poor man out of his misery, I reach for his collar, tug him to me, and press my mouth to his. Breaking away, I nip his lip once more before smiling up at him and whispering, "Show me, Danny. I'm not going anywhere."

His deep inhale, and firm nod, confirm that he just needed reassurance that I wasn't going to run.

Turning from me, he opens the inconspicuous-looking white door and walks into a strange room. It's small, with grey walls and slate floors, and can fit maybe four people. A lone light hangs from the low ceiling but is high enough that the guys don't hit their heads.

Other than that, nothing is in here. Just a round, boring, bland room.

"What is this place?" I am more than curious what he wants to show me.

With a brilliant, smirk, he pushes a small grey section on the wall to my right. It's almost completely flush with the wall and, had I not watched him push it, I wouldn't have known it was there.

He presses his hand against a biometric hand scanner. Three seconds later, a green light flashes from the light above, and a loud whirring sound stirs from behind the wall across from where we entered.

Suddenly, the door swings open and I see a set of concrete stairs. "Holy crackerballs," I whisper in awe.

He chuckles and leads me down the stairs, twisting underneath the house. It takes me longer than I'd like since the stupid cast prevents me from being balanced. That and the curvature of the staircase. But once we reach the bottom, my mouth drops in shock at the sight before me.

A caverneous dungeon fills the space. On one side is a row of four cells. On another is a ridiculous amount of tools hung with black hooks. And, not just tools, but weapons too. Some I've only seen in movies. *How does one get a bazooka? Is that even legal?*

A snort pulls my attention to the middle of the room where a stupidly handsome man is bound, and gagged, to a surgical table. Danny has a remote in one hand and something too small for me to see in the other.

Pressing a button on the remote, Freak by Sub Urban begins to play right before Danny walks over and runs his hand beneath the man's nose.

I shakily take a step forward, eyes wide with a mixture of fear and curiosity. *They said they were mercenaries, right?*

"Alright, Shitbag," Danny announces. "Time to wake the fuck up." The man on the table snaps to attention, his eyes wide and bloodshot. A wet patch forms around his crotch area and Danny scrunches his nose in disgust. "Really, dude? Not in front of the lady."

He chuffs in annoyance before turning to me. "Beatrice, I'd like to introduce you to um... Hmmm. I don't remember. Let's just call him Jackass."

I look between the two of them before concentrating on Danny. Biting my lip, I contemplate my next question. "So, what's he here for?" I go for nonchalant but my voice still wavers. I'm still not totally sure these guys aren't complete psychos but, I'm here now. And, maybe this is why Stu didn't bat an eye when helping me.

"Danny pats the man, roughly, on top of his face as he explains. "This man," he says with a sneer; his eyes truning almost completely black. "And his recently departed friend, like to pretend to be submissive trainers, claim to be Doms, then blow through women's safewords and torture them like sadistic pricks."

He turns toward me, eyes filled with vulnerability as he shows me the beast within. "You see love, I want you to know me. I, too, am a sadistic prick. But, only to those who deserve it. I want you to see me, all of me, and that includes this part, too."

A gentle smile and nod are all I can muster before wobbling over to him and pulling him in for a sweet kiss. "Still not going anywhere," I whisper.

His smile is breathtaking and blindingly beautiful as he scoops me up and kisses me again. This time, though, I feel it all the way deep into my core.

Breaking away, our breaths mingle together before he steps back, pulls a knife from his back pocket, and flips it over; angling the handle toward me. "Shall we?"

The question catches me off-guard, but it also fills me with so many emotions that I can do nothing else but gently take the knife from him, and plunge it into the guy's crotch.

"We shall."

~CHAPTER 26~

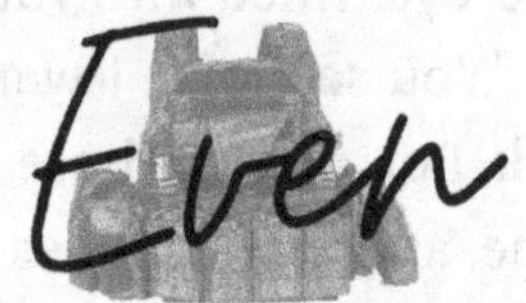

I've been trying to work out these nerves in the gym ever since Danny kissed me before heading to "pick up Bea". Goofy bastard really is trying. And, I think it made me fall harder for him.

A cramp in my leg startles me and I jump off the running mat of the treadmill. Yanking the pin from the treadmill, I vaguely process the treadmill shutting down, but I'm more focused on the pain shooting through my calf. *Fucking bitch-ass bastard. That hurts!*

Breathing through the pain, or trying to, I bite the inside of my cheek and squeeze my eyes shut.

Finally, after at least two minutes, the pain subsides and I hobble off the treadmill. I'm not sure how long I was running for, but the jelly-like feeling in my legs tells me I may have pushed too hard.

Once I make it to the fridge we keep down here, I swipe a water, and chug the whole thing in one go. Tossing it in the trash, I turn and grab another before flattening myself on the mats.

I spend a couple of minutes letting my body cool off. I really should have done a full cool-down but, my God, my legs may never work again.

Eventually, I roll myself up to sitting and go through a series of leg stretches. The pain ebbs and flows through both legs but I focus on the stretch; knowing it's safer than skipping it.

Once I'm done, I roll on shaky knees and push myself to stand; still slightly out of breath as I finish my second water. Looking at the clock, I see that it's been a whole hour. *Oops.* No wonder why my legs feel like they're going to buckle beneath my weight.

I head down the hall, passing by Bea's room. Her sweet fragrance wafts from the door, now, and I wonder if we'll ever be the same when she leaves us. I mean, this is temporary, right?

Shaking my thoughts free, I groan and grumble up the flight of stairs. Once I hit our bedroom, I strip out of my disgusting clothes and pop in the shower. A few buttons later, and a waterfall of bliss falls down from the heavens. *Damn, I love this shower. I'd love it more if Danny and Bea were here with me.*

My cock swells, but I refuse to touch myself. Nope. The next time I cum, it's going to be with Danny or Bea. I need them like I need my next breath. Besides, a little orgasm denial is good for the soul.

I chuckle to myself and roll my eyes. Unfortunately, I can't get the thought of how Bea's reacting to Danny's "date". It was a bold move to bring her down there and offer to let her help. Charlie nixed the idea, at first, until Danny explained that she's been so open, and vulnerable, with us and we need to do the same. He wanted all the cards on the table.

I think it's more for him than her, though. He's so obsessed already, and the longer she stays here, the harder it will be when she leaves. It's going to destroy him.

Eventually, Charlie agreed that there was no need to hide anything; especially since we're now all working together.

But, that doesn't mean I'm not nervous. What if she has a panic attack, what if she hurts herself? What if she can't stand the type of monsters we are?

Yes, we only take the missions that involve fucked up assholes the world is better off without. But, we're still torturers, murders, monsters.

With a heavy sigh, I quickly run through my shower routine. I need to get down there and see how things are going.

Not knowing is making me crazy.

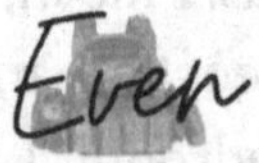

Ten minutes later, I'm silently slipping into the dungeon. A guttural garble is all that can be heard; momentarily causing me to panic thinking that Bea's hurt or in trouble.

But, what I don't expect, is to see her sitting on a stool next to the surgical table, her free leg crossed over her casted leg at the ankle, and her left foot swinging back and forth like she's doing her nails.

I mean, she's doing nails alright, just not the way most women enjoy.

Daisy by Ashnikko plays on the speaker and I see Bea singing out alone, bouncing her head to the beat while she works. Those words from her mouth are insane and hot! She doesn't curse for some reason but, she hits every single word with *feeling* and confidence ... and I can't stop staring.

The pale pink shade of her dress is perfect on her creamy, white skin and her breasts look downright delectable underneath the fabric. The craziest thing is, she doesn't even seem to mind that parts of the white and pale pink striping on the skirt are streaked with blood. Blood I assume isn't hers based on her relaxed demeanor.

I scan the room for Danny and see him gazing at her like she hung the Goddamn moon. His eyes are just a shade darker, hinting that his beast is close, but not in control. Instead, he's leaning against the closest cell; arms crossed over his chest and legs crossed at the ankles. Damn.

"All done!" Beatrice sing-songs excitedly, bringing my attention back to her. "Whatcha think, Babe?" She questions, holding up the man's right hand so Danny can see her work. And, by "work", I mean the perfectly executed slicing off of each and every nail.

She twirls the scalpel she used in her other hand as she waits eagerly for Danny's feedback.

His smile grows wide and he takes a couple of steps forward to assess. "Damn, Flower. How did you make it look so clean? And, how the hell is he still awake?"

She giggles, fucking giggles, and her smile radiates pure joy as she explains. "I take the scalpel and carve a thin layer around the nail first. Then, I work my way from the inside out, as smoothly as possible. It hurts like the dickens but it's more like 100 papercuts instead of 100 knives so, *most* people feel all the pain but never hit their threshold."

Danny picks up one of the discarded nails, twisting and turning it as he inspects it. "That's a clean-ass cut. Surgical, precise..."

He trails off as he places the discarded thumbnail against his own. "Damn, Flower, I could wear this man's nails like women do with nail glue!" He bats his eyes like he's a flirting woman and Beatrice busts out laughing.

Danny stops, his whole body tensing and I ready myself to intervene. Danny misses social cues sometimes and he occasionally mixes up people laughing at him versus with him. I don't think he'll hurt Bea but, judging by the darkness in his eyes, his beast is finally set free.

Bea stops laughing and widens her eyes with a teasing smile.

Within 10 seconds three things happen. One: Danny blindly swipes a knife off the tool tray and plunges it into the man's heart killing him almost instantly. Two: He marches over to Bea, nostrils flaring and breaks the binding off the man; forcing him off the table and onto the floor with a quick shove and a loud *thud*. Three: Danny lifts Bea up and sets her on the table before plunging his tongue into her mouth.

The moan she releases ricochets around the dungeon and my cock hardens instantly. Bea runs her hand through his curls and tugs, just at the base, causing him to growl out. Danny punishes her by taking the fabric of her dress and ripping it down the middle; exposing her nude bra and heaving chest.

Before she takes her next breath, Danny flips the cups down and begins ravishing one of her dark pink rose-colored nipples. He uses his other hand to tweak her other nipple and she thrusts into him.

I palm my cock through my pants, willing it to wait, to calm the fuck down, but I can't help it.

Not with him.

And not with her.

She groans low in her chest. He immediately rises up and surges forward to capture her mouth, as he rips the dress the rest of the way; pushing down the fabric so she's completely naked on top of his steel table.

"D-Danny. Please..." She begs as he plunges one of his long fingers into her tight core.

I feel my cock leaking into my boxers but don't move to alleviate the swelling.

"Please what, My Flower?" He inquires as he lazily pumps his finger in and out before adding another.

She hisses through her teeth and her body ignites; a gorgeous, deep blush covering her from ears to belly.

She is a fucking sight!

Someone groans out, causing Bea to whip her head toward me. *Oops. I guess that was me.*

Danny continues to pump his fingers into her, swirling his thumb over her clit, as he reaches up with his other hand. His fingers grasp her jaw and force her to look at him. "Are you thinking about E fucking you in the woods? Or are you thinking about how my dydoe and pubic cross are going to hit every nerve you didn't know you had?"

She moans long and low, grasping onto his shirt as her knuckles turn white. "Even's going to stand right there. Can he watch, Flower? Can he watch while I pull your first orgasm from you?"

Her whimper is too much for me to bear, so I unzip my pants and free my throbbing cock. I swear it feels like my heart is now living inside of it with the way it pumps to each beat.

I must miss something he does, or says, as she suddenly throws her head back and shouts out her release.

"Good girl." He praises while kissing every inch of her face.

When the waves of her orgasm end, she's leaning her forehead against his, panting for breath. When Danny removes his fingers, she twitches and releases a low groan before staring in disbelief as he licks off her cream. "Fuck, Flower. You make the sweetest nectar I've ever tasted."

I have to hold my tongue from laughing. *Where does he come up with this shit? I've never heard him talk to a woman like this.*

But, judging by the look on Bea's face, she likes his cheesy, dirty words.

CHAPTER 27

I need...I need...I need more. "Ple-ease." I beg, whining petulantly while fisting his shirt. Well, as much as you can with one hand in a cast.

Danny's smug ass smirk is so at odds with his normally playful personality. And, I *am* here for it.

"Whatever you want." He grasps my neck and begins to lower me backwards across the surgical table. Blood still coats parts of my cast and dress but, for the most part, it was a clean, therapeutic session. This wasn't about answers. It was simply blood for blood.

The bite of the cold steel skitters goosebumps across my body as it wars with my overheated flesh. Danny deftly drops his pants and his cock springs free. He's not as long as Stu, thank God, but he's got girth for days. Pair that with his pubic cross and a forking dydoe... *Cheese and rice!*

He wraps his long fingers around the base and begins pumping leisurely. My eyes are glued to his tip as a pearly white bead forms and begins to drop down; disappearing past my view.

"You ready for me?" His voice is husky and possessive.

Dark and delicious.

My pussy clamps down on nothing, causing me to whine as I nod my head vigorously.

"Ok. But, here's the rules."

"Rules?" I squeak out in surprise, snapping my eyes back to meet his.

"Yes, Flower, rules. There are only three. One: You can watch Even but not until I am all the way in. Before that, you're going to keep your eyes on me. I want to watch everything you're feeling through your eyes."

My eyes flutter. Intimacy is so foreign to me. And, quite frankly, terrifying.

Nodding, I quickly give myself a pep talk.

You can do this Bea. It's okay. They've proven, so far, that I can trust them. He was nervous to bring me in here, to share with me. I can do this for him. I can.

OK.

Nodding again, I open my eyes and swallow heavily. "Ok."

I'm rewarded with a sweet kiss and his tip nudging my entrance.

"Number two: If at any point you want to stop, just say so. This isn't a scene, so you don't need a safeword but, just in case, feel free to stop it. No hurt feelings. No further expectations. Deal?"

I nod fervently and smile wide at this caring, sweet, amazing man.

"Good girl." As soon as he says that, his tip breaches my entrance and I gasp in shock. The stretch is a beautiful edge of pain and pleasure but, at the moment, I have to breathe through the pain part. *Holy forkballs it's wide.*

He grits his teeth and shakes with, what I hope is, difficulty holding off on slamming into me.

"Good, good." He chokes out.

After a few deep breaths, his nostrils flare and he focuses his hazy gaze on mine. "Number three: Keep your hands above your head. I want to watch those titties bounce as I fuck you into this table."

"Oh God!" I scream as our gazes lock. He slams balls deep into me just as I raise my arms. I have no choice but to leave the casted one straight. But, the other arm bends and my hand grabs hold of the tray behind my head.

And then...

He fucks me like he's trying to personally imprint his dick into a molded fitting of my vagina.

I can feel his dydoe hitting my g-spot with every thrust. I sort of feel the pubic cross but, not as much as the dydoe. That's normal for me, though. My clit loves to play hide and seek and she's a moody bitch.

Once I have that thought, he moves both of his hands, rests them on my thighs, and opens me wider. The new stretch causes his pubic cross to hit my clit with every thrust and I see the whole damn galaxy.

An orgasm rushes through me, forcing my toes to throw gang signs.

Danny pummels me through the remaining waves and I crash back to shore; sweating, but not sated.

Oh, no...I'm ravenous.

"More," I whisper. "Please, Danny. More." I don't know what I'm asking for. This is freakin' incredible but, I don't want this to end. Not yet.

"Good girl. How about we have Even fill that pretty mouth of yours?" My eyes widen as I remember Even's been watching us this whole time.

Feeling a wave of nervousness, I turn toward Even and find his face tinged with blush. His palm roughly jerks his cock as he watches the spot where Danny and I are connected.

"Crackerballs. That's hot."

I didn't mean to say it out aloud but, when his eyes snap to mine, I see his feral smile grow. And holy cannoli, it's hotter than him watching us.

"Love, please come give Bea something to do with her mouth, will ya?" Danny grits out.

As Even steps forward, he whips off his shirt and tosses it on the ground. His muscles glisten with sweat, dripping down the lines in patterns that I would love to trace with my tongue.

A growly chuckle erupts from him and he bends down to meet my eyes. "Maybe next time. Now, be a good girl and take my cock while my boyfriend fucks your cunt."

My eyes roll in the back of my head at his dirty words. When I moan, his cock appears at my mouth. I eagerly lap up the sticky pre-cum dripping from his magic cross piercing, before sucking it into my mouth. He growls and thrusts deep into my mouth, causing me to gag horrifically.

Withdrawing immediately, he starts to apologize. But I stop him by reaching out my arm and digging my fingers into his taut ass; forcing him back into my mouth.

And, then, they set a brutal pace.

Even quickly learns that I have an awful gag reflex and is careful while thrusting into me; ensuring that his cock doesn't make my puke.

Been there, done that, not wanting a repeat performance.

Danny's cock hits every nerve inside, and outside, of me while Even thrusts eagerly into my hollowed-out mouth.

I don't use any fancy moves. I just suck and suck and suck.

My core tightens and I flush in embarrassment as I hear the squelching sounds coming from my mouth and pussy. My body is overwhelmed with sensations as Danny begins grunting with each thrust.

Even murmurs, coos really, sweet words but I can't process them because Danny slams into me one final time with a roar, rotating his hips so his pubic cross rubs in circles around and on my clit. *Forget flowers.*

He's the flower.

I'm the flower.

We're all forking flowers!

My scream echoes around the dungeon as I clamp down on Danny's fat cock, milking him for all he's worth. At the same time, Even empties himself into me and I greedily, although hazily, suck down every dang drop.

A cold wet cloth wipes away the mess of Danny and my combined releases, jolting me out of my post-orgasm bliss.

Danny chuckles as a bottle of water with a straw sticking out suddenly appears in front of my face. My eyes are bleary as I blink away the tears that I wasn't aware I released.

"Drink, Baby Girl." Even firmly commands. I don't even second-guess it. I obey immediately, swallowing half a dozen gulps before releasing the straw and thumping my head against the table beneath me.

If this is what it's like to be in a shared relationship, sign me up.

~CHAPTER 28~

It's been four weeks since Beatrice's accident. Four weeks since we spent the most incredible, and terrifying night with her.

Four weeks.

Danny, Stu, and Even have all made great strides in their relationships with Beatrice. They sit on the couch almost every night and giggle, flirt, eye-fuck each other.

And, I'm here.

The outside man.

And, I'm not totally sure if I should try or not. I mean, she seems happy enough. She has three of them. So, what do I bring to the table?

A fear of being touched.

Intimacy issues that rival hers.

Paralyzing flashbacks of Cammy every time I see a bathtub. I mean, I tore out the tub in my ensuite the moment I moved in. I couldn't stand to see it.

And, every time she has needed help in the bathroom while I was there, I struggled with not dropping her and running out of there.

She's better off with just them. I'd just be something to pull her down. The others don't have the hangups I do. They're good for her. Yup.

I scrub my hand across my gritty face. I really need to shave, but, we have our first big mission as a team tonight, and I just can't be bothered to.

Bea's healing well, but she still has both casts, so she's staying behind to be our eyes and ears. Stu's been working non-stop while showing Bea how to access and run programs and making sure all of the security feeds inside, and outside of the bakery are up and ready for her.

I swallow the lump in my throat as I think about leaving her here unguarded, but, we need to get this guy, and there are so many blind spots that it's better to take a full team than leave Stu behind like we usually do.

Still, I wish Bea was coming.

But, I also don't.

I growl in frustration at my own wishy-washy emotions and abruptly push myself out of my chair.

Walking down the hallway, I hear their voices- my family, my friends, my gi...*No, not mine.* I quickly shake my head, needing to focus on the task at hand and not how much I wish I could be different.

Be more.

Be better.

Coming to a stop in the living room, I see that everyone is gathered with wide smiles on their faces. Even is sprawled out in Stu's chair. Danny and Stu are standing a couple of feet in front of him, next to Bea as she nuzzles into Stu's chest. My own chest squeezes in discomfort as I fight off jealousy and longing.

Clearing my throat, I clap my hands together, causing them to all whip their heads toward mine. Stu and Danny both grab ahold of Bea's hands and I breathe through the irritation that I can't do the same.

"Alright, Bea, you understand what we need and how to proceed." Her expression is fierce and determined as she nods confidently. "Yes, sir." She says firmly. There was no undertone of sexuality but, damn, my cock jumped like a horny bastard.

"Right," my voice rose a whole octave and I feel my face blush as Stu's lips tip into a knowing grin.

"So, we head out in three minutes. Danny, you clear the main bakery, Stu and I will tap into the secure doors leading to the rooms beneath it and Even, you'll be our point in the back back. Any questions?"

Everyone shakes their heads in acknowledgment before I turn on my heel and stomp toward the bathroom.

I gotta piss before we do this and, honestly, I don't want to see them all lovey-dovey with her and all the bullshit. I just can't.

After taking care of my needs, I wash my hands and splash some water on my face. Looking up at the man in the mirror, I don't even recognize him. His eyes are dark and lifeless, his hair is unkept and longer than my usual buzz cut, and the bags underneath each eye must weigh ten pounds each. He's a mess.

I'm a mess.

I close my eyes and think about the mission, running through the plan in my head a dozen more times, before swinging the bathroom door open and trudging down the stairs.

Beatrice is standing there in her loose jean shorts and one of those damn shoulder shirts she loves so much. Her little tattoo on her collarbone plays peek-a-boo and I both love and hate it.

Giving Stu one last kiss goodbye, before Danny whispers something in her ear, she turns to me, blushing and beautiful. "Um, be careful," she says sincerely. "All of you,"

I swear she burns a hole right through my eyes as she delivers the last line. "Come back to me." She says almost bashfully.

She's looking at me, but I know she's talking about them. They have her heart. I'm not even sure what I have anymore.

With a final nod, I whistle out and we head to the garage. Nighttime has long since fallen and the bakery should be just about closed so, hopefully, Danny won't have to fight to get the remaining stragglers out.

We're all decked out in head-to-toe black, including the balaclavas we'll pull over our heads when we arrive.

I raise the garage once we've all piled in and start the SUV. The sounds of weapons being checked and readied echo throughout the car as we all check our supplies once more.

Stu passes out the coms and we all place them in our ears. "Alright, Alpha signing on."

Then the others chime in, "Bravo on", "Delta on", and "Tango on. Let's Party!" Danny whoops with a laugh, causing everyone to chuckle.

"Omega on." Beatrice's sweet voice filters through the com and I tense up. I didn't realize that my call sign was the same one I used during our fantasy videos. *Shit.*

I slowly turn and glare at Danny who's smiling like he just found the winning lotto numbers. "What *Alpha?* She needed a callsign, too. Might as well fit in with ours. If you know what I mean." He winks exaggeratedly causing Even and Stu to burst out laughing. Unfortunately for me, Beatrice's sweet tinkling laugh echoes through my brain louder than theirs, forcing me to control my urge to knock him straight the fuck out.

"Whatever" I grumble. At least she feels part of the team.

She had a hard time, at first, giving up the information she knew about Franco. For someone who loves vengeance, she has a soft spot as wide as the Grand Canyon. She felt bad for the small-peckered fuck but, in the end, she agreed he would be the most useful to get what we needed. It also helped that we had his rap sheet filled with over a dozen charges of inappropriate behavior towards women.

Of course, he wasn't convicted of a single one. The Crimson Knights have deep, deep pockets and no morals at all.

A few days ago, she reached out to the man himself and asked to meet again. Said she had missed him and sent him a picture of her cleavage. Apparently, he's a tit man.

Although, Danny didn't give two shits about the mission after that. He bent her right over the table and fucked her ten ways from Sunday to "reminder her that she was, and always will be, ours."

Theirs. I've got to remember that.

When he did that, right in front of us all, I stood stock still; as if I could just evaporate into the wall. And I watched, completely entranced as her creamy skin flushed. Her cries of pleasure echoed around the kitchen as Even ruined her clit and Stu gagged her on his cock.

She ended up squirting all over Danny, the table, and the floor; just like at The Raven Room. And, fuck it was hot.

But, I just watched, with a boner that could stop an 18-wheeler in its tracks.

Once they all flew over the edge, I quietly slipped away to relieve my damn self. Then, I hid in my room for an entire day.

I'm pathetic, I know. But, I just can't figure out how to get past my hang-ups with her.

Beatrice's voice breaks me out of my memory as she says, "Four minutes out. Two people near the back. Three people inside the main level."

"Got it sweet thang. Now, can you please put some 'Go' music on?" Danny jumped up and down in his seat excitedly.

He always loves to have music playing right before we get to a mission location. He says it helps get him in the mood to fuck shit up. I don't care either way, but it can be nice to let out the nerves before an operation.

"You got it. Anything in particular?" Bea asks sweetly. "Nope, just something that's going to get my blood pumpin'."

After another second or two in silence, I shit you not, this crazy ass woman plays The Four Tops most known song: I Can't Help Myself (Sugar Pie, Honey Bunch).

And, we all burst out laughing.

"What?" She playfully complains. "I think it's fitting, no?"

Stu begins singing completely over the top, as if Beatrice was here to see him serenading her. Danny and Even join in soon after. Shaking my head, a smile gracing my lips, I focus on driving us towards the bakery.

When it ends, Beatrice giggles uncontrollably. "OK, OK. I'll behave. This one may be a better *motivation* of sorts."

We all wait with bated breath as she cues up the final song before we reach our destination.

Loud music buzzes through our comms, causing me to jump. It's definitely not an old 60's jam. Instead, Rhianna's Birthday Cake plays, and the car charges with another type of energy.

I picture Bea's smug smirk as she sings the provocative words, all but guaranteeing the four of them will have a happy ending after tonight's festivities.

The song is short and sweet, suddenly enveloping the SUV in charged silence. "Thirty seconds. Still two in back, and three up top." She purrs seductively, sweetly, and I shift in my seat as my hard-on presses painfully against my zipper. Damn woman's going to kill us all.

But, shit I love it.

"Roger that, Omega." My voice is huskier than I intended but, judging but the sharp inhale and tiny squeak she releases, it affected her at least half as much as she affected me.

And, I call that a win.

CHAPTER 29

Hearing Charlie's "Alpha tone" sends shivers down my spine and straight into my toes. Dear Lord that man could convince me to do anything he asked; maybe even cut off my own arm.

Delicious.

Decadent.

Molasses.

I have to concentrate on keeping myself in check and focus back on the mission. If not, I'm liable to go run to my room and grab that damn flower Even loves to use on me. *Cheeky Butthead.*

Even's voice breaks me out of my head just in time to hear that they've arrived. I suck in a deep breath and slowly exhale. Then I get to work.

I pull up the alarm systems and plug in the code Stu made for me so I can disable any technical security systems. I wait for a moment as the code tracks what it needs before pinging loudly. "Got it. Bloodlines down."

Danny responds, "Damn that's hot," before a smacking sound reverberates through my earpiece and he yelps. I chuckle, knowing Stu or Charlie probably whacked him. He's always getting into trouble.

"Green is a go," I state clearly and watch as they all appear on a security feed from a nearby shop. It's already been hacked and is currently looping a recording of the empty, dark sidewalk, instead of my men running in front of it.

I watch as Danny takes off towards the front, tucking his gun behind his pants, and walks in the door, smiling wildly.

I watch as Even rounds the back of the bakery and kills the two men guarding the back door; his silencer making it impossible for anyone nearby to hear the shots.

I watch as Stu and Charlie press themselves into a crouch near the wall and wait for Danny to walk the remaining bakery team out; telling them there was a gas leak in the area and he needed to clear it. One of them tripped an alarm before walking out with Danny but, it was disabled...so, no one was alerted.

And then... then, I watch as Even enters the back, Danny joins the others, entering the front, and I lose them all. Every last one vanishes from any security feeds.

And all I'm left with are the comms.

Hours. Hours pass without a word, a breath, a sound.

Ok, maybe not hours, but it felt like that; before all Hell broke loose.

Shots are fired, sounds of glass shattering and men cursing fill my ears and my mind provides me with absolutely horrific images based on the grunts, groans, and *thunks*.

A grunted curse comes from Charlie and I break my silence. I was trying so hard to leave them be; I didn't want to distract them, but I needed to know what the fork was happening.

"Alpha! Delta? Someone!? What is going on!?" My voice is high-pitched as panic takes root.

After a few more grunts and yells, Danny roars, "Fall back! Now!"

My eyes go wide as I hear the raw fear in his voice.

"Go, go, go!!!" Stu screams. Suddenly, a flash of movement brings my attention back to the screens in front of me.

Out of the bakery runs one of my guys with a man over his shoulder. Two others are holding up a third who's limping. They look to be dragging him more than anything.

Stupid Balaclavas. I can't even figure out who is who.

Just then, the man that is being carried, rolls his head back and shouts a curse, "Fuck!"

No, no, no, no. This can't be. I know that voice!

"Ch-Charlie. Oh God, Charlie, are you ok?"

He mumbles something incoherently and I feel a warm tear slither down my cheek.

"Omega, call Doc. Tell him we have two and we need a lot of meds." I nod vigorously as if they could see, and pull up Doc's number. Clicking on his name, I put it on speaker just in time for a harsh orange glow to balloon out before the video feed goes dark The comms rumble with the sounds of what must have been a forking bomb. Then, they screech loudly, before turning to static... then cut out completely.

I scream out.,"Nnnoooooo!!!!"

Panic consumes me, clawing at my throat until I fall to the floor.

Gasping for breath, my world becomes fuzzy before a voice cuts through the haze. "Beatrice! Beatrice! What's going on? I'm on my way but I need to know. I need you to take a breath, can you do that for me?"

I nod, forgetting he can't see me before gulping in mouthfuls of air. "No, no Beatrice; deep breaths. Ready, count one, two, three, hold. Now release." I follow his instructions three more times until I finally come back down.

"OK, sorry. Um, Charlie's hurt, and some other guy but then there was an explosion and I don't know, Doc. I don't know!" I'm spiraling, hyperventilating again, but Doc stops me and forces me to breathe deeply, once again.

As soon as I'm in more control, he gives me instructions to prepare for their arrival.

For the next ten minutes, Doc has me running around the house gathering supplies. But, half the stuff I'm pretty sure was just an excuse to give me something to do; something to take my mind off of the what-ifs swirling around. Like, *why does he need a spatula? And do I really want to know?*

No, I probably don't.

Just as Doc gives me another order, the front door bangs open, startling a shriek from me.

Then, my four bloodied and bruised men limp through the door; having already stripped off their balaclavas.

Well, three of them do.

Even brushes past me looking pissed as all heck while Danny and Stu drag Charlie in by his arms and legs. "Oh, God. Charlie. What the fork happened?" I yell as I hobble behind them toward my bedroom. I don't comment on their choice as I assume they're taking him there because it's the closest one to the door.

Maybe that's what they used to use the room for.

A bitter chill runs down my spine as I realize that Charlie isn't moving. He's barely even groaning while they maneuver him through the house.

I watch helplessly as they hoist him into the bed and begin stripping off his boots. Not knowing what else to do, I hurriedly make my way over to the bed, scoot myself up using my one good arm, and begin looking him over.

He has cuts and gashes along his face and what appears to be road rash down his right arm. His black, long sleeves are shredded, but it's the worst on the right side.

"Help me get this off," Stu says in a shaky voice. His hands are trembling as he fumbles with the velcro of the Kevlar vest.

Danny bumps Stu over a little, swiftly unfastens the vest, and slides it out from under him. Charlie's agonizing groan causes a sob to burst from me and I immediately find the dark, wet spot that's causing him pain; directly to the right of the spot the Kevlar was protecting. It looks like he was shot from the side, and it dug into his chest neat his heart.

Danny wastes no time in ripping the shirt down the middle before ripping both sleeves, as well; letting them lie open and dirty on the bed below.

"Ch-Charlie?" I whisper as Stu starts to pack the wound.

His face is ashen, pale, and covered with sweat. "M-My sweet Omega. I-" His cough breaks through his labored breathing.

I impatiently point toward one of the cold pots of water and fresh cloths Doc requested. But I can't seem to find the words to tell anyone what I need.

Thankfully, Danny interprets my silent request. He rushes over to one of the large pots in the corner, picks it up, and swipes a cloth from the dresser. When he returns, he slides it on the nightstand next to me. I deliberately ignore his rueful smile because I just can't handle his sadness right now.

Wearing my own miserable smile, I dip the cloth in the water and start rubbing the cool liquid across his cheeks, his forehead, then against his scalp.

"Sshhh, it's okay. You're going to be ok. Doc's coming. He'll be here soon." I'm not sure if my rambling is more for me or for him but I can't stop the twin waterfalls sliding down my face.

I should have made more of an effort with him. He was so hot and cold when I first got here. Then, he said he had feelings for me…then he went dark-ish. He hung out with us, and even watched more than one of our little trysts, but he never spoke, never participated, and never stayed in the room if I was by myself. *Maybe he changed his mind.*

Honestly, I'm totally fine if that's the case, but that doesn't mean I don't care for the big grump.

A cold, clammy hand meets mine and I'm shocked out of my head. "Guys…" Charlie's breath rattles and blood has trickled out of his mouth.

"I need," *cough; deep breath*, "a minute."

Confusion racks my brain as I look up to see a devastated Stu. I rip my gaze from his to Danny's and find resignation and a sullen stare. "N-No. They need to help. I don't have enough strength to put pressure on the wound. I can't, I can't…"

Deep breath. "Beatrice, Baby," *deep breath,* "Please. Breathe," *deep breath.*

A sob rips from my soul as I stare into his once icy, blue eyes. Now, they're almost pale compared to the redness streaking around his cornea.

Danny and Stu slip from the room and Charlie pulls his shredded arm around me, forcing me to snuggle up next to him with my head on his chest. I can't even be excited about seeing him half-naked. It's not right.

None of this is right.

He groans and shakily lifts his other arm and places a meaty finger under my chin. He encourages me to look up at him, even though I fight the gentle pressure from his finger for a moment.

"P-please, stay with me, Charlie. You can't give up." His eyes fill with tears as he smiles the sweetest dang smile I've ever seen.

"The only regret..." he hoarsely whispers, "Is that I never took you out on a date."

My tears fall faster and his beautiful, dirty face blurs in front of me.

"I love you Beatrice." *cough- cough; deep, rattling breath.*

He gently urges our lips together and electricity shoots through me in the most horrifically beautiful way.

There's no way. This can't be happening. We didn't even get to start...

Breaking the kiss, he coughs again, blood flying everywhere. After a couple of deep-ish breaths, he barely breathes out, "M-My, little, Omega."

His eyes close. His body relaxes and his hand falls away from my face.

Then the floodgates of tears are ripped open; just like my heart.

~CHAPTER 30~

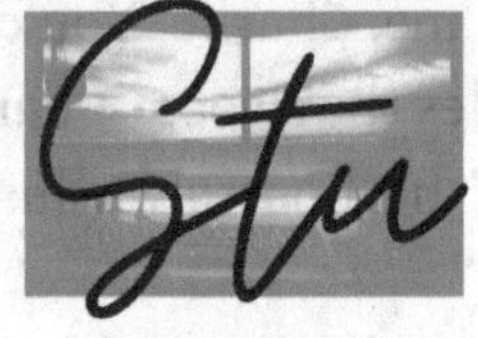

Two Weeks Later

Things have been, well, rough. And not the usual kind of rough. Beatrice has been a pissed-off kitten far more than she's been a purring one. Charlie dying in her arms, especially after admitting he loved her, broke something deep inside of her.

Now, she's a one-woman mercenary team. In fact, she begged Doc to take off the casts so she could get out there and get her revenge. The X-rays looked good, and she has very specific exercises she has to push through each day, so Doc agreed.

She's been a force ever since.

"Queenie," I sing-song to get her attention. She's curling the dumbbells, blaring Little Girl Gone by Chinchilla.

Fitting.

"Beatrice, baby, come on. You've gotta eat something or all that work will be for nothing." She sighs and rolls her eyes in annoyance but drops the bells to the floor; wincing as she stretches and rolls her arms.

Walking over to her, I take her arm in my hand and slowly knead the muscles; relishing in the way her head falls forward and she moans out.

"You are the very best," she mumbles in bliss.

"Yeah, I know. I'll be sure to tell your other boyfriends that you agree." I dance out of her reach just as she goes to swat me with her free arm.

Chuckling, I bend down and plant a big, wet kiss on her lips. "Ok, pretty girl. Up you go. We gotta eat before we get this show on the road."

Absent-mindedly, Bea walks over to the speaker system and turns it off. The silence is deafening and I see that look cross her eyes. The one that tells me she's about to fall apart.

Reaching my hand out, I tilt my head toward the gym door. "Come on. Let's get you cleaned up and fed." She nods solemnly with a far-off look in her eyes as I lead her upstairs to my bathroom.

It's not as fancy as Danny and Even's, but it'll definitely be worth it. My nozzle detaches and has a nice little massaging feature that I have yet to introduce her to.

Stepping into the space, she immediately strips down, no longer worried or nervous about her perfect curves, or the way her thighs' little hot pockets rub together. And, I can't help but smile at her progress with, not only us, but herself.

I strip down to join her, silently watching as she turns the water on and sighs heavily as the hot water beats down on her. Brushing up behind her, I put my hands on her waist, and slowly guide her to face me. She looks... tired. Like, the weight of every decision, both good and bad, is weighing on her shoulders.

"Let me help you," I whisper into her ear before licking the shell. Her answering moan was exactly what I hoped for.

Reaching up above her, I pull the nuzzle out of its grip and switch the setting to a pulsing beat. Her eyes widen before she smiles sweetly. "Please." She whimpers as her legs widen for me.

With a smirk I lean in and kiss her, slowly requesting entrance to her mouth. She gasps when I flick my wrist and begin exploring her wet, warm folds with my free hand.

Plunging my tongue into her mouth, I control the pace and am rewarded with a deep, low, groan vibrating through her chest.

I circle her clit before plunging two fingers into her hot, needy core; her pussy clenching around me like it can't bear the thought of losing me.

"Oh my God! Stu, Yes!" She pants between kisses.

As my fingers fuck in and out of her sweet pussy, her juices trail down my hand, and mingle with the water raining down on us. Her mewls and moans have my dick leaking but he can wait. Right now, it's all about my Queen Bea.

"You gunna come for me, my Queen?" I inquire with a raspy voice.

Her brain must be overloaded because all I get is a simple nod as her pussy begins to clamp down on me.

I bend down and suck a nipple into my mouth right as I flick my other wrist and turn the pulsating water from the nozzle straight to her clit.

Her screams echo around the bathroom, and her head slams against the tiles, as she rides and writhes against my fingers.

I keep up the brutal pace, already feeling another wave starting. Her hands move toward my head as I lap and bite her nipples. "S-Stu!" Her stuttered shout bounces off the walls again and I can't help the grin that takes over my face.

When her body begins to recoil, I move the spray of the water off of her clit and lazily continue to fuck her with my fingers.

Standing back to my full height, I lean in and kiss her with the same languid strides of my fingers.

With a final shudder, I release my fingers from her pussy and bring them between us so she can watch as I stick my long tongue out and lap at her juices. "Best honey I've ever tasted will always be yours, Queen Bea," She groans at my corniness, letting her head fall to my shoulder as she giggles quietly.

Eventually, we do actually get cleaned up. But, I take my time soaping up her hair, and her body. I also refused to give in to her pouting about not letting her take care of my hard-on. That can be saved for later...

When it's time to celebrate the eradication of the Crimson Knights.

CHAPTER 31

Stu always knows how to pull me from my head. As I leave his room, in nothing more than a towel, I mentally prepare myself for the night.

Tonight, we all get freaking revenge. And, one way or another, I'm sending these Crimson Knights straight to Hell.

I pad toward Danny and Even's room, since that's where I've been keeping my clothes. I can't stand to be within three feet of my old room after what happened with Charlie and I refuse to go down there until we're through with these jerkoffs.

I'm still sore but, I'm doing a lot better. However, putting on tight, black jeans is still no easy feat. My leg is giving me more problems than I wish to care about, but I keep that to myself.

After I finish dressing, making sure I pull on a black hoodie over my Kevlar, since nothing else would cover it, I slide on some black combat boots the guys have had me training in. They're big and bulky but, kinda cute actually.

Not that I need to worry about that right now but, hey, a girl's gotta feel some type of way before going out and handing grown men their own behinds.

I brush out my hair before putting it into a high, messy bun. Then I gallop down the stairs before finding the others in the living room.

With a wide grin, I look over my sexy as-sin men, all in black, and take a deep cleansing breath.

"Alright. Let's do this." I announce. For some reason, they're allowing me to take point on this little, ok big, operation.

I turn on my heel to head to the garage.

Halfway there, I suddenly stop and turn. Marching over to each of them, I slam my mouth against theirs; demanding, punishing, passionately. Each one tries to lengthen the kiss but I break away and move on before they can; despite The hilarious protests from Danny.

Turning back around, we head for the SUV. Even and Danny are in front, while Stu and I climb into the back.

After another weapons check, we pull out of the garage and drive into the night.

The car is filled with silence, and I take a moment to remember the events that led us here- to finally finding the Crimson Knights' clubhouse... And to, hopefully, ending them tonight.

Charlie's heart stops beating underneath my ear. I feel it. I know it.

I tried CPR for longer than necessary but I just couldn't apply enough pressure because of my stupid cast.

At some point, Doc had come in. I couldn't hear him or see him. I was completely engrossed in trying to revive Charlie.

Someone grabbed me around my waist and carried me screaming from the room. At the time, I didn't know it was Even. Heck, I didn't know it was him until he flopped me onto his bed and locked us in the room.

Then, I beat the crap out of him. Well, as much as I could.

Have you ever tried pounding a brick wall? No? Well, it hurts. Bad.

Eventually, he wraps his arms around me and collapses with me to the floor. He lets me cry, lets part of my soul die, and just lets me feel.

I remember waking up sometime later in their bed...alone. Then it hit me. There was another man.

I ran as fast as I could, almost falling down the dang stairs. I blamed my cast but, really, I shouldn't have been moving that quickly. I knew better. I just didn't care.

I needed to get to the basement.

I was more than relieved that Danny had Stu set up my biometric information in the system after our first date.

Once the door opened, I dang near hopped down the steps, until Danny and Franco came into view.

Franco.

Franco had definitely seen better days. His left eye was completely swollen shut and it looked like he was drooling a long line of blood, instead of spit. His clothes were torn and tattered from what looked like knife slashes.

Actually, he looked like he'd been in a slasher flick...as the victim.

Once his eyes locked on mine, though, I knew: he was no longer Danny's victim. Nope, he was mine.

It took me less than ten minutes to get the information we needed. While Danny got a lot of information about shipments, plans, and things like that, I only had one question that I needed an answer too: where does the boss stay?

By the time I was finished, he had one missing eye, thanks to a tomato corer and scooper, no finger or toenails, and three needles stuck through his ballsack.

Through and through.

After the third one went in one side, and out the other, he finally talked.

I stood up, turned on my heel, and headed out.

My next stop was finding Doc. He needed to cut these dang casts off so I could head over to their Knight's little hidey hole and kill every last one of them.

Of course, Doc made me wait until after we got another X-ray and made me promise to do the exercise regimens to rebuild the muscles.

Then, the jerks I call my boyfriends made me wait for a "plan". Said I couldn't just go in like Kill Bill and start slaughtering people. I rolled my eyes, but eventually gave in.

Now, we're on our way to finally dole out some vengeance. My heart is still broken, but anger has been a great substitute for sadness.

I'm sure that will change once we're finished. So, until then, I'm riding the anger wave as far as it lets me.

Danny turns around to face me, passing me an earcom with a sly grin and a wink. I raise my brow in question but put the comm in without a word.

Looking over at Stu, he's also smirking at me like he knows something I don't.

"OK, out with it. What's so funny?" Even chuckles before he presses his comm into his own ear at a red light.

"Bravo on." Danny and Stu follow up with "Tango on," and "Delta on." Taking my cue, I respond, "Omega on."

Closing my eyes, I breathe deeply and roll my shoulders.

Right before I hear, "Alpha on."

Air backs up into my lungs and my eyes feel as wide as small tea plates. "Ch- Um, Alpha?"

I feel a lone tear slide down my face as I swallow a lump that's formed in my throat.

"Hey, Omega. Kick some ass for me, yeah?" His voice is gravelly and pained, but, it's him. It's my Charlie.

"Wh-when? How long? Turn around! We need to go home!"

Even's eyes meet mine in the rearview as Danny turns to me with a soft, reassuring smile. Stu grabs my hand, causing me to turn and face him. "He's ok. Doc's with him. He woke up this afternoon while you were in the gym. But, he didn't want you to know yet. He's awake. His vitals are good, but he needed more rest. And, we knew you'd want to be with him but, the best place for you is right here with us while he gets some rest."

Anger at them, and excitement for Charlie, battle each other in my head and my heart.

"Hey, Omega." Charlie's voice shivers down my spine and tingles in my tone.

"Yes, Alpha." I murmur like a well and truly chastised child.

"Ready for your 'Go' song?"

"M-My 'Go' song? What do you mean?"

A round of low chuckles fills the comms as I look between the three in the vehicle with me; completely perplexed.

"Yes, Omega. Your 'Go' song. You're running point." With a wide smile, I feel my heart beating with gratitude and, dare I say, love.

"Ok. Let's do this."

As soon as I finish, the first line of American Horror Show by Snow Wife.

And, my smile turns into a devilish grin.

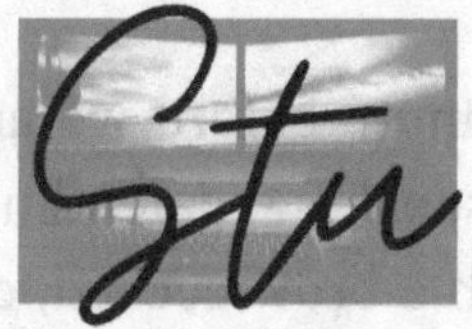

CHAPTER 32

Beatrice's grin is the sexiest, yet, scariest thing I've ever seen. Even scarier than Danny's. But, it doesn't take long to see her truly in action.

The abandoned warehouse that the Crimson Knights hang out in is in a dingy part of town. However, many of the surrounding warehouses are still used to hold merchandise and other products for retailers in the next town. So, it's not unusual to see vehicles and large trucks coming and going.

Even loops around the block once, so that we can get a decent look at what they're doing since there were no security cameras in or around the warehouse that we could tap into.

By the looks of it, they're having a huge party. Scantily dressed women and dozens on dozens of men are hanging inside and outside of a large, open loading dock.

"There. At the top." I point out the main bastard, sitting at the top of the loading dock like he's the king.

Even nods, then drives off to park in an alley a couple of streets down.

I glance over and see Beatrice chewing on her cheek. "What's in that beautiful brain of yours, my Queen?"

Danny turns around to look at her with brows raised in question.

"I want to go in myself."

We all shout out against the abhorrent idea. It's completely preposterous.

It takes another minute before we are all quiet enough to realize that she's not speaking, defending herself, or anything. But, she sits there with a brow cocked, chin raised high, and a sly, sexy smirk on that beautiful face.

"Oh shit. Is this the point where she kicks our asses before going after the bad guys?" Danny's eyes glitter in amusement under the street lights and I hear him chuckle softly.

"Omega, you've got it. Give 'em hell."

We all groan because Charlie's word is law, and he just made a decision.

"Thanks, Alpha. Now, listen up..."

Ten minutes later, we're all sportin' hard-ons as Beatrice steps out of the SUV, now parked only a block away, and struts down the sidewalk. While she explained her new plan, she shimmied out of her sweatshirt and, with a lot of pushback from us, her Kevlar vest.

She tore her shirt diagonally at the top to make it hang off of her delicate shoulder and tucked the front part into her black, skintight jeans, then hopped out.

We watch, holding our breaths, as she starts waving toward a group of women hanging near the entrance of the warehouse. Other small groups are coming and going so it doesn't look strange for her to just be walking on up.

It seems like one of them hands her a beer, that we see she pretends to sip on, before they all head into the warehouse with her.

We silently watch, mesmerized by how seamlessly she seems to have fit in with the crowd.

The leader, the main douchebag himself appears to be following them in and Even releases a low growl. "Omega, the King is in."

She doesn't respond, obviously, but it sets us all on edge; not being able to see what's happening inside. Not being able to keep our eyes on her.

I'm bouncing my knee so hard that it feels like I'm shaking the whole vehicle.

Even glares at me in the mirror and I realize that I am, in fact, shaking the whole vehicle.

Danny's flicking his knife over his knuckles and I rub my sweating hands down my pants.

"Where's the bathroom?" Beatrice's sweet voice comes through the comms, finally. We decided she'd turn it on only when ready in case there was some kind of metal detector.

"Sweet, thanks." She tinkles out.

"Six bedrooms, one living room, a meeting, room, and a bathroom with a communal shower? This place is huge!" She giggles like a schoolgirl at a man's response; although, we can't hear it over the noise in the room.

"What's that room?"

We wait, as silently as possible as she cues us into what she's seeing. "An armory? Oooo, How cool! That must mean you can protect all of us, right? I mean, only real men know how to use those big, scary guns."

Her fake-as-fuck flirting is nauseating and my eye twitches as I wait for something, anything, to let us know that we need to go in and help her.

The leader is flirting with my girl and I just may go crazy listening to her flirt back; even if it is pretend.

Two women giggle before their voices echo around them. A toilet flushes and the sound of water turning on makes the comms sound staticky but, soon, it clears again.

We can hear how the sound changes from one room to another before she coos, "Oh, how chivalrous."

"Yes, please. But, I need to make a quick call. Stay in here and wait for me, ok? I'll be back in one minute. Promise." She says between what sounds like someone kissing on her.

I heave in my seat, having to open the door for air. I know she has to make this seem real but, I'm not a fan of anyone touching what's ours.

A door clicks before she snickers, "See ya, Dirtbag."

"Dirtbag, Baby girl? Dirtbag? Why is it that you don't curse again?" Even laughs loud and long, making Danny and I wince. We almost miss Bea's quiet response.

"Jerkface number three thought women shouldn't curse. He had super fun ways to punish me. Some habits die hard." She may be whispering but the memory clearly caused her pain. I'm so dang glad he's already pig food.

Danny growls deep in his throat and Even chuffs in annoyance.

"Hey, my Mom called. Apparently, she's super sick. I'll see you next time." She says happily.

Less than five minutes later, she's sashaying back to the SUV, a confident look on her face and a strut that won't stop. Damn, she's fine.

And mine. *Ours.*

Sliding into the car, she shuts the door, takes in a deep breath, and looks at us all with raised brows. "What?"

"God dammit, woman. Why do you have to be so fucking hot all the time? No more missions for you. My dick is pressing into my zipper. Any longer and it's going to unzip my jeans for me." Danny bitches, shifting in his seat as he palms his cock.

She laughs out, shaking her head, then looks over at me.

"The leader is waiting in his room; which is next to the armory. His device should go off when the armory one does so, no matter what, we know he's taking care of." She says with a vengeful smile.

Biting on her lip, she leans over, presses a kiss to my cheek, and whispers in my ear, "Push the button."

"Anything for you my Queen." I click 'enter' on my keyboard and watch as cockroaches scatter.

Literally.

Bea put a small explosive on the armory door. Large enough to cause some damage, but not so large that it should seriously injure someone.

But, all the same, it clears every innocent out of the building and has all the members rushing in.

"Bye, bye boys." She says, just as I hit 'enter' on the last group of bombs. The bombs may be small, but they give off blasts large enough to cave in whole rooms.

Which is precisely why she stuck one to each and every door knob she passed from the entrance to the back of the warehouse.

We watch in awe as the building lights up like a giant firework.

Dozens of men and women run screaming from the chaos.

Suddenly, another set of blasts goes off, causing Bea to yelp in surprise. Danny cackles like a lunatic and claps his hands. "There goes the rest of the armory." He rejoices.

Before anyone can see the vehicle, Even puts the SUV in drive, and heads back home.

"All clear. We're coming home, Alpha." I announce.

We all lean back in our seats, Bea grabs hold of my hand, and we relish in the silence of victory.

~CHAPTER 33~

Charlie

I end up falling asleep before they make it home. These pain meds are no joke. And, I guess my body was still tired after being in a coma for two weeks. *So strange.*

When I do wake up, the scent of eucalyptus and lavender fills my nose and I feel a smile cross my face. I try to hold my groan in as I open my eyes and shift toward her scent.

When I finally look over to my right, I am both relieved and perturbed to see her there. Relieved because she's here, but perturbed because she's not touching me. I mean, I know that I've more or less- ok more- shied away from touch. I know she's caught my muscles tensing or the cringe I can't hide when someone pats me on the shoulder, or when she tries to rub against my hand or arm. It's no one's fault but mine. However, after dying in her arms, I'm done.

She's the one. And, I've spent far too long allowing my hang-ups to stop me from being with her.

Biting my cheek, I slowly inch toward her, wrap my arm around her, and pull her into me. Pour girl is passed smooth out. In fact, her sigh of contentment is the only sign she's even alive.

Her beautiful, heart-shaped face is relaxed and peaceful. There are a few freckles on her face that I never noticed before and her lashes are perfect little wings, fanning out from her eyelids.

I inhale her sweet scent and close my eyes, just letting my body get used to the feel of someone against me, someone's warmth seeping into me... And the longer I lie there with her, the more comfortably I feel; the more comforted.

Some time later, my eyes pop open as Beatrice wiggles out of my grasp. "Where do you think you're going?" I cough as each word scratches my overly-dried mouth.

She jumps before turning her face to me; ocean blue eyes wide with what seems like nervousness with a hint of fear.

My brows pinch together, "What's wrong?" I rasp.

She quickly slips off the bed, and I love to see her without her casts for the first time in 2 months. The guys told me that Doc removed them, before the mission, but seeing it, seeing her... is perfection.

A cup of water with a straw appears in my view and I come back to myself. Sucking in a few greedy gulps, I feel the cooling sensation flood my body. I don't even realize I'm groaning until I hear her giggle. My eyes pop back open, to find her cheeks flushed, her hair a wavy mess from sleep, and her eyes twinkling with so much damn joy that it makes my heart expand almost painfully.

"Hi."

"Hi." She responds with a chuckle.

Nothing else is said for a whole ass eternity but, it doesn't matter. I can see the feelings, the thoughts, the hope shining in her eyes. For the first time since I met her, all of her walls are down. She's completely vulnerable, completely open, and allowing herself to completely feel everything. *Good God, it's glorious.*

"Can I take you on a date?" The words slip from my mouth before I can stop them, causing my eyes to widen in surprise; along with hers.

"Um, yes, but, I think you have a couple more days of bed rest before you can get up. Your bullet wound is just about healed, but you needed a full transfusion when you slipped into the coma. So, maybe this weekend? If you promise to keep it low-key?"

I smile wide, more excited than I think I've ever been as I hold my hand out to her. She looks at it for a moment before slowly finding my gaze with hers. Then, she gingerly slides her hand into mine and lets me intertwine our fingers together.

With matching smiles, she snuggles up against me, and we spend the rest of the evening talking, making plans, and watching *Lucifer.*

CHAPTER 34

It's only been a few days since we blew the Crimson Knights to kingdom come but, we haven't had much downtime. A few nearby warehouses had gone up in flames so HQ had a lot of butt-kissing to do with the local government. *Oops.*

Firefighters had extinguished the flames by the next morning. Since then, clean-up crews have made quite a dent for their efforts.

Still, the Knights have been taken care of and, bonus, a major Cartel player was also there so, win-win.

But, tonight, we finally get some time off. And by we, I mean Charlie demanded that he and I make time for our date now, rather than later.

As I look at my reflection in the mirror, I see a huge smile, lightly blushed cheeks, and wide, bright eyes. I can't tell you the last time I felt so good, so beautiful, so...*loved.*

I straightened my hair, allowing the, now, brunette locks to flare a little around the shoulder. I went with a deep green dress that ombres down to the bottom until it turns white. It has a smattering of tiny white spots all over the dress; like little tiny stars sparkling in the night. Although, my favorite part is the deep V-neckline that shows off a healthy amount of cleavage.

The green looks great against my pale skin and brunette hair but, I had to add a little brightener and thicker eyeliner just to make sure I didn't wash my eyes out.

A knock on the door startles me from my perusal and I rush over to throw on a pair of nude ballet flats. My leg, and ankle, cannot handle heels any longer so flats and Chucks are about all I can get away with now.

I swing my bedroom door open, now having taken my room back over, and see Charlie standing there in a slate grey button-up, rolled up to his elbows, and a pair of dark blue jeans.

His black shoes compliment the whole ensemble but, what makes me smile the most, is the way his mouth is gaping open as he drinks me in. "Damn, Baby. Warn a man before you open the door next time. You're a vision in green." He murmurs the end, as if he didn't mean to say the last part, then smiles and presents his elbow to me.

I chuckle and whisper "Thank you," as I thread my arm through his and allow him to take me away.

I don't miss the fact that he only, sort of, winced from my touch, but he kept his arm steady as we walked through the house and into the garage.

"Where are we going?" I inquire as I slip into his beautiful metallic blue Ram 3500. He closes the door for me and rounds the car quickly. He turns on the car and fiddles with his phone before placing it in the phone holder with a map pulled up.

Once his seatbelt is clicked in, he opens the garage, puts the car in reverse, and grins at me. "Somewhere not here," he chuckles. I feel myself do the same and wiggle in the seat; the leather cooling some of the heat rising inside of me.

As we back out of the garage, he pushes a button on the steering wheel, and Take Me to Church by Hozier begins to play softly through the car.

"Tell me something about you, Beatrice."

"Like what?" I answer confused.

"Anything. Something true, something real, something personal. We spent so much time skirting around personal topics. I want to know everything. All the good, all the bad, all the boring."

My cheeks heat at his words and I have to force myself to breathe deeply to prevent myself from shutting down. That was my go-to mode for so long, that I have to consciously make the decisions every minute of every day to be open. To let myself feel.

Swallowing audibly, I try to comb my brain for something he doesn't already know. And then, "My three birds tattoo is from *Divergent*. When Tris got it near her collarbone, I wanted it right away, because I wanted to be her. I wanted to be *Divergent*. I wanted to be strong, selfless, courageous, brave, smart, and honest. I wanted to be someone my mother could be proud of, a person would want to be friends with, a woman a man wanted to be with. Instead, I became a chameleon. I put on masks based on the group I was with. I molded myself to be what I knew they would accept, like, maybe even love. And, after a while, I couldn't figure out who I was anymore.

Going after my abusers gave me some of myself back, which is why I closed myself off to everyone. It wasn't just about the fear of being hurt. I was afraid I'd lose myself after years of being the perfect chameleon. And, I didn't want to be that anymore."

Charlie doesn't speak but takes his hand, grabs mine, and returns it to the shifter. He then intertwines his fingers with mine; his hand resting on top of mine, as he shifts through the gears and drives us to our destination.

After a comfortable silence he blows a raspberry and proclaims, "That was a lot more truth than I expected but, Beatrice, I'm glad you don't want to be anyone other than you. We see you, just as you are, and we love you because of that. *I* love you because of that. I get the fear of being hurt. Unfortunately, my hurt is just a little different."

As we wind through the streets, he explains what happened with his ex, Cammy. How broken he was, how he didn't feel good enough, how it pushed the need to stay in control and not be touched.

At the next light we come to, I unbuckle my seatbelt, lean over, kiss his cheek, and look at him with every ounce of love I can muster. "Thank you. I'm sorry I scared you, I'm sorry I hurt you. And, no, those feelings are no longer there. You guys have changed me in so many ways. Supported me, let me just be myself, laughed and loved with me, and I couldn't possibly ask for more."

His smile is so bright that I melt into the leather, and grin the rest of the way to the restaurant.

After the most amazing homemade chips, queso, and guacamole, we took an order of sopapilla cheesecakes to-go. Then, Charlie made his way to a nearby park that has been long forgotten.

"I can't believe I've lived here for so long and never knew this place existed."

Charlie swallows the mouthful of his dessert before responding, "Yeah, a buddy of mine bought it a few years back. Turned it into a nature preserve because of the animals and foliage in the area. Unfortunately, suburbia built up around it, so it quickly became overshadowed.

I nod, remembering the small, gated entrance we drove through before the lot opened up into a huge wooded area. Had I not been curious to see where we were going, I would have totally missed the turn in; which was tucked in between two sprawling neighborhoods.

We walked a few dozen yards into the wooded area and found a beautiful clearing with a quaint little pond. We sat a couple of feet away from the edge and dug into our desserts before I broke the silence.

"Thank you for bringing me here. It's hard to believe sometimes that beauty still exists even though there's so much darkness around us."

I was speaking more of our past than present but, before I can add that comment, he responds, "*You're* the beauty to our darkness."

His rough voice forces me to snap my gaze to his. There I find sincerity, want… need.

I don't know if he moves first or if I do, but we're suddenly mouth-to-mouth. He controls this kiss and I am powerless to do anything other than submit. Submit to him with my body, my heart, and my dang soul.

My core tingles with awareness and I feel my panties dampen immediately. He rolls on his back, lifting me like a ragdoll and positioning my aching clit right on top of his jean-clad cock.

It's so big, that I can feel every ridge as I shamelessly grind on him; needing the friction more than I need my next breath.

"I need you, Beatrice. I need you now."

I moan at his words but shake my head immediately. "No, not Beatrice." I whimper.

Charlie growls beneath me. "Is that what you want, Omega? You need your Alpha to make you cum so hard you see stars?"

I whimper, riding his jean-clad cock as he pours out his filthy words. "Please," I whine impatiently.

"Take my cock out, Omega. Take it out and see what's yours."

I briefly pause, taken aback by his words; or *word*. "Mine?" I whisper.

He surges up, cradling my ass with his large hands, and whispers against my lips, "Yours, Omega. Just like you're mine."

He slams his mouth into mine and steals my tongue from my mouth.

I groan, thrusting my hips before clawing at his buttons, desperately trying to get his cock free without breaking our kiss.

Eventually, the dang button unclasps, and I zip his zipper down so fast I almost catch my own finger.

But, with a little finagling, I finally free his long, beautiful cock. It looks even better in person than it did through the computer screen. A perfect drop of pre-cum leaks from his tip and drops down his Prince Albert. His head is dang near purple while his shaft is the most delectable shade of fair pink. His lorum piercing sits about half an inch below his shaft, through his ball sack, and dear God it's so hot that I lick my lips with anticipation.

"Not this time, baby. I need you now." He reaches under my dress, rips my panties off of my body, before lifting me up and plunging his rod straight into my clenching, needy pussy.

"Holy forking cannoli-based crackerballs." He's too big. I think I've been split in two. This will be the worst ER experience ever if I have to go in for stitches because my boyfriend tried to kill me.

"Oh, shit, Goddamn woman. You're squeezing me so tight." His chuckle sounds more pained than pleasurable. But, I can relate.

Totally, completely relate.

A few deep breaths later, my body finally gets used to the large dick occupying it. And, then, the damn bursts.

I rock against him vigorously. Roughly grinding my clit against his pelvis with every thrust. It feels so good and my toes begin to tingle with my impending orgasm.

At least thirty seconds later, maybe more, and I'm still on the razor's edge.

Charlie's being so wonderful, he's groaning and his breath hitches every time his piercing bumps against my g-spot.

It feels so dang good but... *Gggrrrr*.

Finally, I give up on chasing an orgasm I can already tell won't happen. Switching it up, I lean forward, push him to lie down, and slam my lips against his.

He moans into my mouth; the new angle making my eyes roll as this piercing hits every dang spot inside of me.

Wanting to make sure he gets a good orgasm, I tuck my legs against his and start raising my ass until just his tip, and the forking piercing, are inside of me before bouncing up and down his length.

His eyes roll back and I grin as a look filled with pain and pleasure crosses his handsome, chiseled face.

I learned that leaning forward and bouncing, basically twerking, my rear on top of a guy uses my thighs more than my knees; something that saves my poor, crappy knees from considerable pain.

I can also bounce faster than when I'm using my knees so, *bonus.*

Within moments Charlie's groans turn into grunts and his mouth disconnects from mine.

He squeezes my hips and begins to thrust upward every time I bounce downward. The movement causes my eyes to cross and I scream out as pain and pleasure mix like a tasty cocktail deep inside my core.

After a few more thrusts, he bottoms out and holds me there. With a roar, I feel his warm, sticky cum splashing deep into my womb; again, and again, and again.

His hands squeeze my hips a little harder, then he releases, letting his head fall back against the grass as a look of pure satisfaction and relaxation converges over his face.

I sigh contentedly and nuzzle into his neck, placing feather-light kisses there as I slowly rock against him; completely addicted to the way he feels inside of me.

Not even ten seconds later, I can feel him growing harder inside of me. I lift my head and look into his ice-blue eyes, giggling at the mischievous glint I see there.

With a cocked brow, he smiles and rasps, "Did you really think you were going to get away with not orgasming?" He finishes with a growl and flips me on all fours faster than I can comment.

Then, his dick slams right into me from behind and the ball from his looped lorum piercing hits my clit, causing me to scream, "Oh my Jesus!"

He doesn't even give me a moment to adjust. He just starts slamming into me, his piercings hitting every damn spot inside, and outside, of me over, and over, and over, and....

Fireworks burst behind my eyelids as I scream out my release.

Eventually, my arms give out and I half-face plant into the grass beneath me, but I'm too enraptured by my orgasm rolling like waves crashing into shore.

At some point, he finishes, again, and pulls out of me. I hiss out a breath and he groans in response. He then rips off his shirt and cleans me off; almost making me beg for another round.

Unfortunately, I don't have any time to ogle him properly as he maneuvers me into his arms, acting as big spoon to my little spoon.

And, we spend the next hour or so just talking, wrapped in each other's arms, watching the sun set behind the trees.

~CHAPTER 35~

Almost Three Months Later

My lungs are on fire and my breaths are sawing in and out of my chest at an alarming rate. The air is thick with humidity, yes even in February, and the sun is just about to set. Not that I can see much as I sprint through the forest. With the various Oak trees and the gorgeous Loblolly Pine canopy looming over me, this forest is creepy as shit. But the *men* behind me...

Thankfully, it's warm today since I'm running through the forest; the same one I met Even, as E, just over 6 months ago. But, this time, I'm wearing a Red-Riding Hood cape, red lingerie, and my new red Chucks. I'm basically a giant target; but I love it.

Who knew Valentine's could be so fun with four masked men chasing after you?

A snap sounds out somewhere behind me as a crunching of leaves echoes out to my right. *I have to go. Now.*

I'm coming up on the same bridge I got caught at last time so I bypass that, hoping this chase can last a little longer.

Hoping the high can last a little longer.

Adrenaline and fear threaten to choke me as I man with a Jason mask, striped red, and wearing all black clothing, steps just into my path a few feet in front of me; kind of like in the movie.

I scream out and immediately turn left, hoping to outrun him.

My heart beats in my ears, impeding my ability to hear anything around me. So, I keep running.

I'm pretty sure that working out has increased some of my energy, and endurance, but I'm definitely not built for this much running.

My arms are pumping and sweat trickles down my spine, but I keep going until I see a clearing off in the distance. I'm just about to breach the treeline when a man in a COD mask and full gear steps directly in front of me.

"Hello, Baby girl." His deep, sexy voice momentarily stuns me. But, I'm able to recover from my initial fear and immediately turn around, running head-first into a man dressed up as Ghostface.

"Where you going, Queenie?" His voice rumbles from behind the mask, causing my naughty bits to tingle with anticipation.

"Um, uh, that way." I stammer, just before fleeing to my right. You know, just in time to be boxed in by a Punisher mask.

"Forkin' A!" I screech.

Two pairs of hands immediately land on my body; two on my hips and two on my shoulders. "Oh, my little, red flower. You're shaking." Danny coos beneath his mask.

My pussy clenches with need and a whimpered cough comes out. *Dang, I need to exercise more. These little stunts are going to kill me.*

But, oh! What a way to go!

My brain finally overrides my body and I remember I'm supposed to fight. "P-please. Let me go."

A growly chuckle behind me vibrates through my body and I recognize Charlie's deep, molasses voice slithering down my body. "Sweet. Little. Omega. Already begging." He coos mockingly.

"Don't mock me," I huff as I push back and wriggle against him, trying to dislodge his large hands from my shoulders.

He just chuckles like a big jerkface so I change tactics. I spin left, then right, quickly before ramming my body into Danny, shoving him out of my way.

I hear Stu and Danny's maniacal laughter follow me as I sprint through the woods.

Satisfaction and pride fill me and I mentally high-five myself.

But, that's short-lived.

A thick arm snakes around from behind me, plucking me straight off the ground before turning me around and slamming my chest into a nearby Oak. A loud "Oomph" pushes all the air straight from my body and I cry out in pain as the bark scratches against my skin.

The arm retreats long enough to grab me by the hair, just at the base of my neck by the roots, and I scream out, "Leave me alone you, you jerk!"

A chorus of chuckles echo around me and I know I'm done for.

"No! Let me go. Let. Me. GO!" I scream as I try kicking off of the tree to release his hold on my hair.

Suddenly, a warm, wet tongue licks a path from the base of my neck to my earlobe. It disappears just before nibbling on my ear; the warmth of his breath matches the sweet, icing-like nature of his sexy voice. "Never, my Flower. Never," He whispers before my wrists are clasped tightly in two different hands.

My body shivers as I'm lifted away from the biting bark of the Oak tree in front of me.

Before I can process anything, I'm shoved roughly over a fallen tree stump, rump high in the air as course ropes are tied around my wrists, then around a tree about two feet in front of me.

My wrists chafe as I test the bindings. Tears stream down my face as adrenaline and fear wrap around my throat and squeeze.

"P-please." I cry, wriggling around.

The long, hooded cape is unceremoniously ripped from my body, allowing a cool breeze to caress my skin, and causes my nipples to tighten.

Two large hands, with long-lean fingers, caress my naked rear; my cheeks only being separated by a single string from my thong. They slide, smooth, grope, squeeze and I feel myself grow wetter than I ever thought possible.

The hands disappear and a loud smack reverberates through the air leaving my ass feeling like it's on fire.

I scream out, just before two fingers slide from the top of my crack, loop underneath my thong strap, and continue their path down before plunging into my core. The *squelch* that rings out should be embarrassing, but I can't care because it feels so damn good.

Within moments, I'm a bumbling writhing mess as the rough bark cuts into my belly, the ropes burn my wrists, and the fingers inside my needy pussy corkscrew in and out of me.

"Oh, God. Oh, Please!" I beg.

"Please what, Baby Girl? Does this needy little pussy need to cum?" Even's muffled voice mocks me, and if I wasn't so sure his fingers were inside me, I would snarl.

Male laughter filters around me as Danny responds, "Easy, Love. Sounds like my Flower's about to grow thorns." He jabs.

Then, I do snarl.

And his dang fingers leave me.

"What the actual for-" I'm cut off from my sudo-expletive as a rough hand palms my throat and forces my head upright; bringing my eye-to...tip, with a huge cock.

Charlie growls out a hoarse, "Suck." And, I do.

Greedily.

The moment I swirl my tongue around his thick, pierced tip, two fingers plunge straight back into my soaking pussy.

I mewl as I melt into the rhythm they set. When the fingers slide in, Charlie's cock slides out. When he slides back in, bumping the back of my throat, I gag as the fingers slide back out.

Charlie learned my gag reflex issues early, just like that rest did, but he still likes to push. And, I can't lie, I like it when he pushes. He knows what will happen if he pushes so far. *All too well.*

But, he takes it all like a real man; with apologies, cooing affirmations, and lots of orgasms.

Just that thought alone causes an orgasm to rip through my body and I scream out as Charlie continues to hammer into my mouth until he comes with a shout; spilling all of his cum deep inside so I can swallow every last drop.

Hands gently stroke my body, my hair, my arms, my rear...

I blink out of my orgasm-induced stupor just as the ropes are cut from my wrists. I don't know how, but I want more...

I need more.

"Please," I whine, petulantly as I wriggle in Danny's grasp. He chuckles in my ear as Stu strips off the long, black Ghostface cover-up and tosses it to the ground.

"You ready, Bea?" Stu asks.

I look into his pale blue eyes and am filled with so much love and excitement that, I know whatever they have in store, I'm down for it.

With a subtle nod, I reach for Stu and allow him to guide me to lie on top of him. He steals a kiss from me and I let him gently explore my mouth passionately and filled with more love than I know what to do with.

He doesn't break the kiss when he nudges his tip into my entrance.

He doesn't break the kiss when he pushes the first few bar-bells in.

And, he doesn't break the kiss when I moan out as he thrusts balls-deep into my pussy.

Our bodies mold together, almost too sweetly, before Even whispers into my ear. "Baby Girl? You gonna let Danny into this tight pussy with Stu?"

"What?" I screech.

We've double penetrated before, but not there. Never there. "It won't fit!" I voice out my concerns; now shaking with fear and anticipation for totally different reasons.

"He'll be gentle. And, if he's not..." He trails off, licking a line up my neck and up to my ear before adding, "I'll fuck him as rough as he fucks you."

I groan and dig my nails into Stu's chest. "Dammit." Stu spits. "You like that, don't you, Bea? You like the thought of Even fucking Danny while Danny helps me split you in two. You're strangling my cock here, Bea." His whine almost makes me orgasm a second time, but, before I can, I tense up at the feeling of Danny's tip meeting my entrance just above Stu's cock.

My eyes go wide and Danny begins stroking my back with one hand while Stu oh, so, slowly moves his hips in small circles.

My breath backs up into my lungs until Stu pushes a hand between our bodies and starts lightly strumming clit.

"Lean forward, Bea. Let him in." Stu whispers as his gaze holds mine.

I take that opportunity to lean all the way forward, chest-to-chest, boobs smashed against his perfect pecs, and snag his lip ring; playing with the loop before tugging.

We groan in unison as Danny's head breaches my entrance and pops in just past his dydoe piercing. "Shit, fuck. Man, damn." Danny curses against my back between my shoulder blades and slowly starts rocking into me.
"Stu, fuck! Your piercings. Good God." He continues.

"Feels good doesn't it, Babe?" I ask cheekily. Then, he slides in a little further, rocking me forward into Stu.

I hiss as pain and pleasure war for dominance before Stu pinches my clit.

The orgasm that takes over my body is brutally intense, and blinding.

Somewhere in the deep recesses of my orgasm-drunk mind, I feel Danny sheath himself fully inside of me...right on top of Stu's cock.

I continue trembling between the two of them as my orgasm subsides.

Just as I come down, I basically flop onto Stu, feeling Danny's cock jump; quickly followed by Stu's.

Danny hisses behind me and I force myself to lift my head up and turn toward him.

Even is kneeling behind him, now maskless and shirtless, and his face is pinched in concentration. "Does he feel good, Babe?" I ask Danny, wiggling around a little, now that my body was used to both of them inside of me.

He hisses out and stutters, "S-s-so good."

With that Even rocks Danny deeper into me. We both moan with the movement and I give myself over to the moment.

All three men quickly get a rhythm as I submit my body for them to use like a good little slut.

Even thrusts into Danny, shoving him into me, which Stu meets. As he slides out, so does Danny; and I assume Even.

In, out, in, out.

It's like they're all fucking me with one giant cock and I may die from overstimulation.

We mewl, groan, moan, and whimper as one sweaty, sensual pile of feelings. I'm pretty sure every nerve ending has caught on fire and I'm burning from the inside out in a blaze of love.

A low, rumbling groan forces my head up and I see Charlie, mask now off, staring down at me adoringly. Like I'm the most precious jewel he's ever seen, palming his hard, again, cock.

"Charlie, please." I pant out. "I need you, too." His smile is so bright, rare, only for me as he steps toward us, kneels next to Stu's head, and thrusts into my waiting mouth.

It takes just a moment for his thrusts to match the others but, pretty soon, we're all in sync. *All together in our love and devotion for each other.*

And that thought sends me spiraling over the edge.

The whole galaxy opens up and swallows my whole as my orgasm splinters my soul into shards.

Beatrice

After passing smooth out on top of Stu, they allowed me to sleep for about ten minutes before rousing me awake, and cleaning me up with something from...somewhere.

We silently head back to the parking lot, Stu and Danny both holding my hands, as usual.

Once we reach the clearing for the lot, our blacked-out Suburban sits alone underneath a lot lamp, like a beacon of rest and recovery.

But first, I abruptly pull away from them and turn around. Danny and Stu both pout while Even looks at me with concern and Charlie starts scanning my body for injuries.

Holding up a hand, I giggle a little before assuring them I'm ok and I just need a moment.

Reaching into the pocket of my, now ripped cloak, I silently thank God that the box is still in there. I briefly forgot about it earlier in favor of chasing the high.

Swallowing the wooly lump in my throat, I cough a little, trying to clear it before gazing between my men.

My sweet, loving, freakishly smart Stu; with all his piercings, pale blue eyes, and tousled hair; now electric blue.

My overzealous, adorable, psychopath, Danny; with his perfect black curls and maple-colored eyes.

My strong, caring, gentle Viking, Even; with his long, soft beard, ridiculously lush hair, and blue-green eyes.

And, of course, my grumpy, gruff, no-nonsense protector; with his perfect hair, ice-blue eyes, and chiseled jaw.

All four, very different men. And all four are absolutely mine.

With a smile I can't contain, I get down on one knee, in nothing more than my skimpy red thong and lacey, red baby doll lingerie.

And, I pour out my soul.

"I spent so much of my life in a defensive position. Eventually, I learned how to play offensively. But, with you, with all of you, I didn't need to play either way. I could just, be." I swallow audibly as I look at Stu first.

"You're friendship brought me back to life. I tried to push you away, but I couldn't do life without you. I love you, all of you, and want to spend the rest of my life, proving you made the right choice of being my best friend. I love you, Stu, with every cell in my body. "

Stu's eyes leak tears and he smiles sweetly at me. "I love you too, Queen Bea."

My eyes begin to fill so I turn to face Even next. "Even, you brought some of my craziest fantasies to life. You fought for me the way you fight for Danny. You've been a hundred percent positive that I belonged to you all far before I would even entertain the thought. And, I thank you. Thank you so much for not giving up on me; even when I gave up on myself. I love you."

Even's smile is so wide, that I have to imagine his cheeks hurt, before he says, "I love you, too, Baby Girl."

Then I move on.

"Charlie, you were one of few who ever saw me, for me. Even when you were a jerkface..." I chuckle with a roll of my eyes, and the others follow. "You were still busy protecting us, protecting me. Even when you were hurting, or needed help, you still put each of us first, put me first, and I can't thank you enough for being there for me. Even when you were mad at me. I love you and I want to be with you every day, for the rest of our lives."

He narrows his eyes a little and smirks; his eyes sparkling with adoration. "I love you, too, my little Omega."

I grin, almost shyly, before turning to focus on Danny last. "Sweet Danny. You once told me that your darkness called out to mine that night we first met. I never told you this, but, I felt it then, too. You are the perfect balance for each of us in this family. You're the enforcer, the comedian. You're silly when we all need to let loose, and you're willing to seek vengeance against anyone who dares cross any of our lines. I need you, just as much as I need the others. But, I love you, because you're you."

"Aw, Flower, I love you, too!" He exclaims and jumps up and down.

Without further ado, I open the long, black velvet box I had made especially for this occasion. The box reveals four, different, black Tungsten bands.

"I'm sorry it took me so long to see you all. To see *us*. But, now I do. And, I know you're it for me. All of you. So, will you, *all,* marry me?" I inquire as tears cascade down my cheeks.

They all look at each other, shifting their heads and gazes back and forth before focusing their attention on me.

They all nod as they step forward. Stu reaches his hand for mine and helps me up off of my aching knee.

"Yes, beautiful Bea. Always, yes. But, um..."

He looks back at Charlie who pulls out a little black box and they all drop down to one knee.

"You always do know how to fumble our plans but, if you didn't, you wouldn't be you. And, we love you. Will you, Beatrice, marry *us*?"

They're a total blur as tears have just poured out of me.

"Yes, always, yes." I bumble like an idiot and dangle my hand.

A gorgeous, heart-shaped diamond sits on top of a black band. Each side of the heart houses two red rubies, signifying my four, amazing men.

They all stand and I shakily remove Stu's band first.

They're all black Tungsten with a thin, red opal inset all the way around. However, they all have something different about them.

I hand each man their rings and encourage them to read the inscriptions on the inside:

"Always Your Queen Bea," is on Stu's.

"Always Your Baby Girl," is on Even's.

"Always Your Flower," is on Danny's.

And, "Always Your Omega," is on Charlie's.

We swap kisses, hugs, and a lot of tears before heading home. Our home.

I don't know what we'll do with my old property, or the rest of our lives, but all I know is: we'll do it together.

A NOTE FROM THE AUTHOR

Hey, Howdy, Hi!
I truly hope you enjoyed Beatrice and her men as
much as I enjoyed creating them.

Thank you so much for reading the Not-So
Childish Games Duet and for all of your support.

Also, a huge shout-out to my bestie, editor, and
beta reader,
Kayla! You are all the things and I am grateful for
you every day.

ALSO BY TRIS WYNTERS

The Consumed Series

DARK REVERSE HAREM/POLYAMOROUS
ROMANCE

See Me

Save Me

Free Me

Not-So Childish Games Duet

DARK REVERSE HAREM/POLYAMOROUS
ROMANCE

Hide, Don't Seek

Tag, We're It

Follow me on Facebook and TikTok for information about upcoming books and overall ridiculousness.
Facebook: https://www.facebook.com/groups/1422660571980693/

TikTok: https://www.tiktok.com/@triswynterswrites

Instagram:

TRISWYNTERSWRITES